EVIL
Fairies
Love
Hair

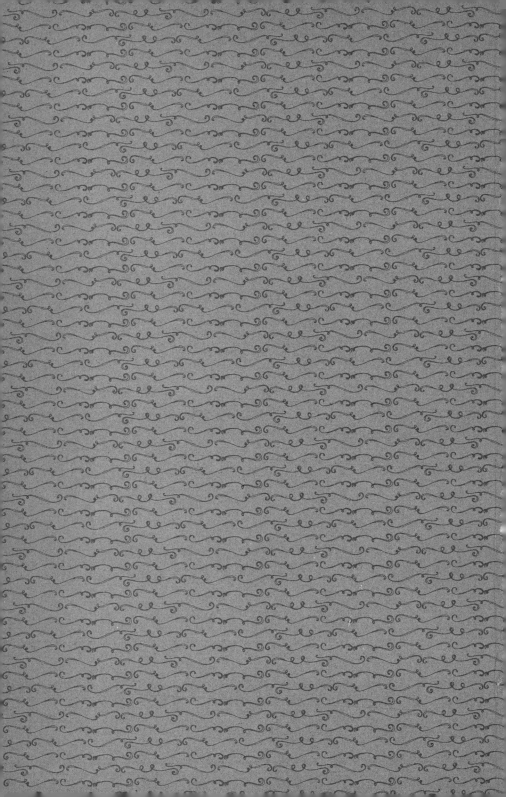

EVIL FAIRIES Love Hair

A novel by **Mary G. Thompson**

with illustrations by **Blake Henry**

CLARION BOOKS
Houghton Mifflin Harcourt
Boston   New York

CLARION BOOKS
215 Park Avenue South, New York, New York 10003

Clarion Books is an imprint of
Houghton Mifflin Harcourt Publishing Company.

www.hmhco.com

The text was set in Minister Light.

Library of Congress Cataloging-in-Publication Data
Thompson, Mary G. (Mary Gloria), 1978–
Evil fairies love hair / by Mary G. Thompson ; illustrations by Blake Henry.
pages cm
Summary: Middle-schooler Ali's wish will come true if she follows all the rules
to grow 100 evil fairies and feed them human hair, then find another child to
do the same, but she is determined to find out what else the fairies are up to.
ISBN 978-0-547-85903-3 (hardcover)
[1. Fairies—Fiction. 2. Wishes—Fiction. 3. Magic—Fiction. 4. Hair—Fiction.
5. Missing children—Fiction.] I. Henry, Blake, illustrator. II. Title.
PZ7.T37169Evi 2014
[Fic]—dc23
2013016273

Manufactured in the United States of America
DOC 10 9 8 7 6 5 4 3 2 1
4500476471

FOR WENDY

AGREEMENT

I, ALISON E.B. BUTLER,

in exchange for one WISH,* hereby agree:

I will grow one hundred (100) fairies.

I will pass on two (2) flock starters to another Child.

I will follow all the rules.**

ALISON E.B. BUTLER

*I understand that I am not entitled to my WISH until the child to whom
I pass my flock starters grows one hundred (100) fairies. I also understand that if
I break any rules, all fairy obligations under this agreement shall be null and void
and Consequences may apply.

ONE

"ALISON Elizabeth Brown Butler!"

"I'm coming!" Ali hurriedly pushed the rest of the dirt on top of the little hill she'd built and packed it down. "I'll be back," she whispered.

"Hurry," said a little voice.

"I will." Ali rubbed her right hand across her neck, making sure she didn't have any stray hairs, and stood up. From here, she couldn't see the evil fairies at all. How was she supposed to make sure they stayed put?

"Al-li-son!"

"I said, I'm coming!" Ali jogged across the backyard and up the steps into the kitchen. Everyone was at the table—Mom, Dad, and Hannah. Dad and Hannah were already eating.

"I called you fifteen minutes ago," said Mom. She picked up Ali's plate and slammed a helping of mashed potatoes on top of a mangled slice of roast beef.

"I'm sorry," said Ali, sliding into her seat. Unfortunately, her seat was right across from Mom's, so she had no way of avoiding the glare. She took her plate and stuffed a spoonful of potato into her mouth, not even bothering with salt and pepper.

"Your mother worked hard on this meal, young lady," said Dad.

"I'ff ffoggy," said Ali.

"You're still wearing that stupid hairdo?" said Hannah. "What is going *on* with that?"

Ali almost choked. She hated being called stupid, and Hannah knew it. "It's not stupid," she said.

"I'm sorry, Ali, but a bun right smack on top of your head is stupid. And that hairspray is disgusting. No wonder you repel boys." Hannah flicked a lock of her perfect, glossy light-brown hair off her shoulder. The blond highlights practically sparkled.

Ali had been planning to raid the shower drain every day for hair, but Hannah was really tempting her. If only her sister knew how much her hair was worth, and what the evil fairies could do. Then she'd have her hair up in a "stupid" bun, too. But no one over thirteen knew about the fairies, unless they were still in middle school, like Michael. When you finished eighth grade, it was over. Hannah was about to finish tenth grade, so she had no chance at all. But Ali had a whole 'nother year. She smiled and took a bite of cold roast beef.

"What are you smiling about?" Hannah delicately lifted her last bite of green beans to her lips, chewed, and swallowed. "I'm going to do my homework." She smiled at Mom and got up from the table. She took her plate with her, rinsed it, and put it in the dishwasher. So perfect. Her parents thought Hannah spent all her time studying to bring home those straight-A report cards. But Ali knew better. "Doing homework" probably meant calling Michael's older brother, Deacon. He was just as big as Michael, and twice as mean—to everyone but Hannah. Actually, he'd been mean to Hannah, too, up until around Christmas, but she'd forgotten all about that.

"Me too," said Ali. She shoved another bite into her mouth and chewed as quickly as she could. Michael had insisted on coming to check up on her, and she didn't want him to get impatient and come in the front door. She rushed her plate over to the sink.

"If you don't want to eat now, you can forget about having a snack," said Dad.

"Fine. I had plenty," said Ali.

"Do you need any help with your homework?" Mom asked.

"No," Ali said.

"Well, with finals coming up, you can always use a boost," said Mom. *Unlike Hannah, who's smart enough to never need help,* Ali heard.

"I can do it myself," she said, and before Mom could say anything else, she ran through the living room and sprang up the stairs. Of course Mom would offer to help *her* and not Hannah. As if Ali were too stupid to figure anything out. Just because she didn't get the same grades didn't mean she wasn't every bit as smart as Hannah. *In fact, I'm smarter,* Ali told herself. *I don't spend all my time fixing my hair.* She barreled into her bedroom and stifled a surprised scream.

Michael was sitting on her bed, tossing her pink stuffed unicorn between his giant hands. He was at least six feet tall, even though he was only fourteen, and his shaved head added to the feeling of *big.*

Ali pushed the door shut. "How did you get in here?" she whispered. "I *said* I'd let you in the back door."

"Well, I let myself in." He grinned, showing two rows of crooked yellow teeth.

That's what you get for smoking, Ali thought. *Gross.*

He pointed the unicorn's horn at the open window. Ali stomped over to the bed and grabbed the unicorn out of his hand. "You're going to kill my tree *and* get me grounded."

"None of that's going to matter once you get your flock grown." He picked up Ali's tuxedo-shirt-wearing teddy bear and started bouncing it.

Ali grimaced. She'd have to wash everything in her room now. "I know, and I'm doing the best I can. I've got the first mound done. Why can't you just go home and wait like a normal person?"

"You know why." He squeezed Teddy Tux's head. "I've got three weeks until eighth grade is over. And if your flock isn't done by then, I lose everything." He was no longer smiling. "You think I don't know what everyone thinks of me? Once I'm the best football player in the country, they'll be sorry."

"That's what you're going to wish for?" Ali had wondered what Michael's wish would be, but she'd been afraid to ask. Michael was the kind of person you avoided if you could. And the tone of his voice right now wasn't changing her mind.

"Well, I was going to wish for better parents, but then I found out that you're only allowed to change yourself," Michael said. Ali had once overheard her parents talking about Michael and Deacon's dad, saying that if he'd ever come home from the bar, maybe his boys wouldn't be such goons. That was one of the reasons Hannah had to hide the fact that she was dating Deacon. But Ali didn't want to show Michael that she knew that much.

"You can wish for happiness," said Ali. "That way you won't care what your parents do."

"Yeah, but I don't want to just be magic happy," said Michael. "If I can be a sports star, I'll be rich and famous, and *that* will make me happy. Maybe I'll do basketball instead of football. I don't know. For sure, though, I'm not going to use my wish for something dumb like being good looking." He rolled his eyes.

Ali rolled hers, too. Michael had gotten his fairies from Jennifer Jackson, who also lived on their street. When Michael had finished growing his flock and had passed the two starter fairies on to Ali, Jennifer had gotten to make her wish. And she'd chosen to be gorgeous. As if she wasn't popular enough already. Why hadn't she wished for something she could really use, like a little bit of brainpower? That was what Ali was going to wish for. If she were a genius, she'd never have to worry about doing homework or studying for tests again, and she'd never get anything but As. She'd never have to see that look on her mom's face after every report card, the one that said *I'm very disappointed in you, young lady.* And most of all, she'd never again have to see that smug look on Hannah's face when *she* brought home straight As and Ali didn't.

"You have nothing to worry about," said Ali. "I've got the directions you gave me. I'll build more mounds, and I'll get all the hair they need. They'll be done in *two* weeks."

"Okay," said Michael, dropping Teddy Tux back onto Ali's pillow. "You know I can't actually help, but I can answer some questions."

"I know," said Ali. "Now get out of here before my parents hear us."

He got up off the bed and headed for the window. He put his hands on the sill, then turned back around. "You read the whole thing, right?"

"Of course."

"Then you know you have to be careful."

Ali patted her bun. "See? Not a stray hair."

"Okay, but it's not just that. I mean, there's a reason everyone calls them *evil* fairies."

"Besides that they climb into kids' brains through their hair follicles and eat them from the inside out?" She crossed her arms over her chest. Sure, that was why all the girls who knew about them wore their hair in ridiculous buns and the boys shaved their heads — the fairies were supposed to be so overwhelmed by their love for hair that they'd climb right up into your head, even if you were the one helping them grow a new flock. But no one could be sure that was what had happened to Molly Parker and Tyler Griswold. Sometimes kids just disappeared.

"So remember that," said Michael. "Grow the flock, get your wish, and get out." Was he actually concerned about her? *Nah.*

"Don't worry about me," said Ali. "I'll be fine."

"Okay," said Michael. With a slight shake of his stubbly head, he jumped out the window and into the tree.

Ali cringed as the branches cracked, but no one else seemed to have heard. She reached for the band holding her bun in place. It was still tight. No evil fairies were going to get *her.*

"Hair."

"Hair."

"She's late."

"Midnight."

"Can't wait."

"Soon."

"Hair."

"Hair."

TWO

ALI pulled the directions Michael had given her out of her back pocket, sat down at her desk, and smoothed the paper. She'd already read them about ten times, but it couldn't hurt to be extra sure. Every little thing had to be right.

HOW TO GROW A FLOCK OF FAIRIES
(2 fairy starter plan)

Keep the fairies in the jar until steps 1—5 are done. They will be banging against the jar and screaming at you, but DON'T LET THEM OUT! Complete steps 1—7 before dark.

1. Find a spot in your backyard where no one will disturb the fairies and where there is a nice soft patch of soil.

2. Dig a square hole exactly 6 inches on each side. **Use a ruler to measure.**

3. Put 3 seashells in the hole. You can use any kind of seashell, as long as all three shells fit comfortably in the hole with at least an inch of space on all four sides.

4. Cover the seashells with a thin layer of grass.

5. Put 4/5 of the dirt back on top of the shells and the grass and pat it into a nice round mound.

Ali had done all that already. The fairies had jumped and screamed and banged against the side of the jar, but she hadn't let them out until she was supposed to.

6. Turn the jar on its head so that the top is touching

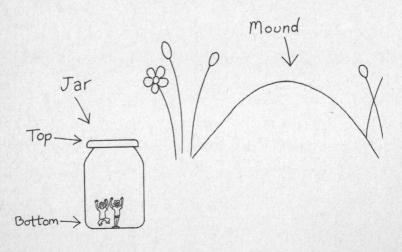

the mound. Then, very carefully, unscrew the top and let the fairies out onto the mound. They will immediately burrow inside. Don't worry, you will still be able to hear each other.

7. Pat down the last 1/5 of the dirt on top of where the fairies burrowed in.

So far so good. She had done all that, and she hadn't needed to look at the picture to figure out where the top and bottom of the jar were. Did the fairies think all kids were stupid or just her? *I may not get straight As,* Ali thought, *but I know which end of a jar is up.*

Complete steps 8—11 after dark, but before midnight.

Ali glanced at her bedside clock. It was only 6:28. It wasn't dark yet.

8. Gather at least a tablespoon of hair for each fairy.
9. Wrap the hair in as many paper towels as necessary, and bring it out to the fairies.
10. Place the hair evenly around the bottom of the mound.
11. STEP BACK!

Make sure you do not get any hair stuck to your

fingers. Remember, your fairies will be ravenous. Do not let the fairies near your own hair!

The directions ended there. Michael had told her that all she had to do was keep following them again and again once the fairies began to multiply. Each set of ten fairies needed its own mound. She smoothed the paper again and glanced back at the clock. 6:31.

Ring-ring.

Crap. That had to be Crista. She grabbed the phone before her mom could get it. "Hello?"

"I saw you wearing that bun. You got them, didn't you?"

"So what? You're just mad because I got them and you didn't."

"No, I'm mad because it's stupid. Do you want to end up like Molly and Tyler?"

"We don't know what really happened to them." Crista was such a fraidy cat lately. She'd quit their soccer team and started wearing skirts. If she got a wish, she'd probably wish to be beautiful like Jennifer Jackson.

"Yes, we do," Crista said. "What's going on with you? You used to be smart and now you're hanging around with Michael Landis. Did you start smoking, too?"

"Of course not. And I'm not 'hanging around' with Michael. He just gave me the starter kit."

"It's not just Michael. You can't really believe that these little creatures you yourself call 'evil fairies' are going to grant you a wish, no strings attached? What are you going to wish for, your brains back?"

"No, I'm going to wish for brains, period," said Ali. "I'm going to get all As all the time. Nobody's going to call me average or think Hannah's the smart one."

"Nobody thinks Hannah's the smart one," said Crista. "The smart one wouldn't be going out with Deacon Landis."

"My parents think so. All the teachers at school think so."

"Then *they're* idiots," said Crista.

Ali didn't say anything. Crista didn't understand. She didn't know what it was like to have everybody looking at you thinking what a waste you were, wondering how someone as perfect as Hannah could have a sister who was so average. Crista was an only child, and she got mostly As, too.

"Ali, come on," Crista said. "You don't need some magic spell. You just need to do your homework. You can already get As if you want to."

"It's not that easy!" Ali cried. She wanted it to be

easy, and it would be once she got her wish. Everyone would praise her and look up to her, and she could do whatever she wanted and never have to work at anything ever again.

"I just don't want anything bad to happen," Crista said. "You're my best friend."

"I know." Ali felt bad for comparing Crista to Jennifer, even if it was only in her head. "I can pass them on to you when I'm done. Then you can have your wish, too."

"I don't have a wish," said Crista. "Except that you'd stop."

"You can't stop once you've started." It was true. If she let the fairies out of the jar, she had to grow the flock to one hundred fairies. If she didn't, something bad would happen. No one knew exactly what, but supposedly Tyler had quit—and where was he now?

Crista let out one of her long, exasperated sighs. "Fine. Do whatever you want."

"I'm—hello?" All Ali heard was the dial tone. Crista had hung up. Of course. Tell Ali she wasn't stupid, then order her around like she *was* stupid, and then, when Ali didn't do exactly what she wanted, get mad and hang up. Well, when Ali finished growing her flock (and got another person to grow a flock), she wouldn't have to listen to Crista or anyone else.

She flipped Michael's paper over. On the back was what was really important—the rules about what you could wish for.

IMPROVEMENT IN:
 health
 appearance
 talent
 mental acuity
 happiness
 likability
 athletic ability
 dreams

Before

After

Likability

YOU MAY PICK ONE ASPECT. DON'T BE GREEDY!

HEXES:
illness
ridicule
clumsiness
ugliness
nightmares
fat

your enemy

HA! HA! HA!

HA!

Ridicule

YOU MAY ONLY HEX PEOPLE WHO DESERVE IT!

They did make "likability" look good. And there had to be someone she'd like to see get ridiculed. Funny how you *could* change someone else but not in a good way—only by hexing them. Well, she definitely wasn't going to waste her wish on a hex. She was going to pick "mental acuity." If she were really smart, surely she could figure out how to make people like her without magic. Maybe she could be a soccer star, too, because brains were a huge part of winning at sports. Michael wasn't thinking his wish through—"mental acuity" was the way to go. Carefully, she folded the paper up again and put it back into her pocket. It was still only 7:00, but it wasn't too early to start collecting the hair. Two tablespoons would be a piece of cake.

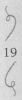

"I have good news, Grand Miss Coiffure!"

"Has another flock come to the fold while I was away?"

"Yes, Grand Miss—three. Three hundred more heads have joined the Kingdome."

"And those three children have all passed on their starter kits?"

"Yes, Miss, all three."

"And have the previous growers made their wishes?"

"Yes, Miss. One beauty, one singing voice, and one hex."

"Which hex was it?"

"Ugliness, Miss. A fine batch of acne and a bulbous nose."

Grand Miss Coiffure chuckled in her hearty squeak.

"Will that be all, Miss?"

"Yes, Lockner. Very good work. Very good work indeed."

THREE

Ali and Hannah walked along in silence. It was a cruel twist of fate that the middle school was a block away from the high school, so Ali had to deal with Hannah for an extra fifteen minutes every day. Weren't evenings and weekends enough?

"I love the way you've done your bun today," Hannah said.

"Shut up."

"No, really. It says, 'Don't worry, Mom, I'm not dating.'"

"A lot of girls do it this way," said Ali, and she immediately hated herself. Since when did she care what anyone thought?

"Uh-huh." Hannah casually patted her painstakingly coiffed waves. The blond highlights cost so much that Hannah had to do all the yard work to get an extra allowance.

"Good morning, Ali." Jennifer Jackson tripped into

the street to go around them. Her hair was up in the exact same bun that Ali had, only she looked like a screen goddess instead of a seventh-grader. There was no way she'd had those boobs before the magic.

"Hi, Jennifer," said Ali. "Bye, Hannah." She split off down the sidewalk toward the middle school with Jennifer so she'd avoid Hannah's inevitable comment, but it floated toward her.

"Bye, Tweedledum. Say hello to Tweedledee!"

"Idiot," Ali muttered. She cast a sidelong glance at the siren walking next to her. "Why are you still wearing the bun, anyway? You aren't going near any fairies anymore, right?"

"I like it," said Jennifer. "Now that I look like this, I can do whatever I want."

Ali had to laugh. Jennifer was probably right. She could come to school in a potato sack and people would copy her. And the best part about the fairies' magic was that if you didn't know about the fairies, you'd never be able to tell the difference—everyone else thought that Jennifer had always been gorgeous. Still, even magic beauty probably faded when you got old. Ali wanted something that would last forever.

Without saying goodbye, Jennifer strode off toward

her gaggle of other pretty girls. Before, she'd been the richest, but now she was totally on top.

Ali turned away. She was not interested in that.

Something was poking the back of her neck.

She scratched it with her right hand.

"Hey, stop that!" The voice was coming from the base of her skull—from her hairline.

She reached back and grabbed the fairy, keeping her fist tight. She held her hand right up to her mouth and whispered. "What are you doing here?" She opened a tiny space between her thumb and forefinger to let the evil little thing explain.

Its head popped out. The head was the size of a large pencil eraser, and it basically looked like the head of a tiny woman. Except that regular women not only weren't two and a half inches tall, but they also didn't have bulging, bright blue eyes that filled up half their faces. Plus, the fairy's head was bald. "Hair," it said.

"I just fed you last night. I'll get you more as soon as it gets dark."

"Now."

"The directions say—"

"That's only the first day," it interrupted. "You have to feed us in the morning, too. Feed us now."

"Okay, I'll find some, just—" There was Crista.

"Stay put." She shoved the fairy into her jacket pocket and zipped it up.

Crista eyed the bulging pocket. "Trouble?"

"No." Oh great, here came Michael, too. Just what she needed. But he rushed past them. A whiff of cigarette odor wafted off him. "Blech. What a loser," said Ali, laying it on thick so Crista wouldn't think she was friends with him.

"Yeah. How did last night go?"

"It went fine. No prob—Ow!"

"What?"

The fairy had burrowed right through Ali's coat pocket and was now digging her nails into Ali's hip. "I feel sick." Ali turned and ran back down the sidewalk.

"Ali!" Crista yelled.

Ali ignored her and kept running. As she ran, the fairy climbed up the side of her body. "Stop! I'm going to get you some. That hurts!" She raced by a pair of straggling sixth graders who burst into giggles. Where was she going to get more hair? She could check the drains, but how much would be there from just one morning? Instead of heading toward home, she took a right and ran toward Fifth Street. There was a hair salon. She'd just run in and grab some and run out.

"Ooooow!" The fairy was up to her armpit, and that

really hurt. She stopped, ripped her jacket open, stuck her hand under her shirt, and pulled the fairy off her body. Some of her skin came with it. "Why are you hurting me? I'm trying to help you. Just calm down!"

"I'm sorry, Alison," said the fairy. "It's just that I'm so hungry when I've started a new flock. I can't control myself."

"All right, it's all right," Ali said. "You're just a baby, aren't you? What's your name?"

"Not a baby, one of the flock starters. My name is Pilose." She blinked her large eyes and pulled her arms out of Ali's fist. She stroked Ali's fingers with her tiny hands. "I'll be calm."

"Okay. Stay in the pocket this time." Ali zipped Pilose in and started moving again. She could already see the salon. There was Mrs. Hopper sweeping the hair along the floor. Ali walked up to the door.

Mrs. Hopper put the broom down and went to answer the phone. Ali ran in, picked up as much hair as she could grab in her fists, and ran back out, and she didn't stop running until she was home and had collapsed on her knees in front of the mound. She dropped the hair on the ground and pulled Pilose out of her pocket.

The second fairy jumped out of the mound and was on top of the hair in an instant. Then a third and fourth fairy jumped out. All four fairies devoured the hair. Apparently it didn't matter one bit that Ali hadn't carefully arranged it around the mound. In less than a minute, they'd devoured every last strand. Then they all stood in a row and looked up at her with those enormous eyes.

Ali was still gasping for breath after her wild run. "What? Is that not enough?" How had they multiplied so quickly? She knew she was supposed to make a hundred, but it had only been one night.

Three of the fairies looked to Pilose, who stepped forward. "Before midnight," she said.

"Where am I supposed to get all this hair?"

"Heads," said Pilose.

"Heads," the others echoed. They all smiled in unison, big pink smiles that filled the whole rest of their faces that weren't eyes.

"Okay. Okay, I got it. You're going to stay here, right?" But before she'd finished speaking, the fairies had all disappeared into their mound. It was as still and silent as if it were just a regular pile of dirt.

Heads. This was going to be more difficult than she had thought. She checked her bun, picked herself up off the ground, and headed in the opposite direction from school—back toward Mrs. Hopper's hair salon.

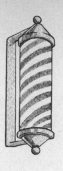

FOUR

ALI peered through the glass door of the hair salon. There were no customers, and Mrs. Hopper was nowhere to be seen. Right in the middle of the floor was a nice pile of hair clippings. This was perfect. She pushed the door open and rushed over to the pile of hair. But how was she going to carry it all home? She looked around for some kind of bag to put it in.

"Well, hello, dearie." Mrs. Hopper was standing in the doorway at the back of the salon. She was holding a large, full black garbage bag and she had a broad smile on her face.

"Um . . . hi," said Ali. "Um . . . do you mind if I take this pile of hair clippings?" For a school project? To make a wig? Why should Mrs. Hopper care anyway?

"Oh, but you can't, dearie," said Mrs. Hopper. Her long, gray hair was partly piled on her head in an unstable, off-center bun, but quite a bit of it flowed down her back, swinging as she walked toward Ali. "You see, this is *my* hair."

"Um . . ." Ali wanted to turn around and run, but that was ridiculous. She'd had her hair cut by Mrs. Hopper since she was a baby. The nice old lady wouldn't hurt a fly.

"Did you think I didn't see you, running in here and stealing *my* hair?" Mrs. Hopper was right over Ali now. She smiled her big smile and opened the top of her garbage bag.

"I'm sorry," Ali stammered. "I didn't think . . . I thought you were going to throw it out."

"You didn't think at all, did you, dearie? Your job is to get the hair we can't get for ourselves. You get *more* hair, the Kingdome gives you your heart's desire."

"The Kingdome? You mean . . ." Ali took a step backward.

"Little tiny harmless fairies," said Mrs. Hopper. The tiny voice squeaked from her large, smiling mouth. Her light blue old-lady eyes suddenly seemed three times larger.

"That's not what I think," said Ali. "I just didn't know."

"Don't worry, dearie," said Mrs. Hopper, speaking in Mrs. Hopper's voice again. She reached out and stroked Ali's shoulder.

Ali shivered.

"You're perfectly safe as long as you get us what we need. Now run along and find some nice hirsute human *heads*." Mrs. Hopper turned the garbage bag over. A large mass of hair clippings dropped out, dwarfing the pile that had Ali had been about to steal. As the hair whooshed down, some of it landed on Ali.

"Hair."

"Hair."

"Hair."

"Hair."

"Ahh! Get off me!" Ali frantically tried to brush the hair off her clothes, but it was too late. Fairies were already crawling on her. Their little hands and feet dug into her clothes. They crawled under her shirt, onto her stomach and back. She brushed harder and shook her body.

"Ow!"

"Stop it!"

"Human wretch!"

"Hair."

Ali ran for the door, slapping her hands against her

body, wiggling her arms and legs, swinging her head. She burst out, not paying attention to which way she was running. All she could think about was getting away. She ran until she realized that she was only a block away from school, then stopped and brushed and brushed herself. Finally, she thought she had brushed all the hair off.

"Hello? Are any of you on me?"

Nobody answered.

She sat down on the curb and put her head in her hands. Strands were falling out of her bun. She'd have to go home and fix it before she went back to school. What did school matter, anyway? Mrs. Hopper was an evil fairy! How could that be? And what were all those other fairies doing in the salon? Were those the ones that other kids grew?

"Ali."

Oh no, I'm in trouble. She looked up, but it was only Michael.

"I've been looking for you everywhere. What's wrong?"

She was at eye level with his knees—really his knees, because his jeans were old and full of holes. "I went to Mrs. Hopper's—"

"The salon?" Michael sat down next to her with a thump. "That's genius! Why didn't I think of that?"

"Mrs. Hopper is a fairy!"

"What? You mean she got tiny?"

"No, she's . . . I think she's been replaced! By a big giant human-looking fairy!" She told him the whole story. "So there are a whole bunch of them living in the hair salon. And they call themselves the 'Kingdome.' Please, can you check my back for any hair I missed?"

Michael roughly brushed the back of her T-shirt. "I don't see any."

"Oh, thank goodness." She squirmed, remembering all those little hands and feet touching her body. "I don't know if I want to do this anymore."

"You have to," said Michael.

"I know. Tyler. And you want your wish. I want my wish too. But you didn't *see* her. She was so weird. It wasn't Mrs. Hopper. Michael, what happened to Mrs. Hopper?" That poor, sweet old lady. Was she dead? Done in by fairies grown by the kids whose hair she'd been cutting her whole life? She didn't deserve that.

Michael pulled out a cigarette. With his large hands and his shaved head, he looked a lot older than fourteen. But his hand was shaking. "I don't know. I never should've gotten you into this."

"You warned me. I'm just stupid. That's why I need a wish. I'm going to pick 'mental acuity.'"

"You're not stupid," said Michael. "You thought of going to the hair salon. And remember when me and Deacon locked you in your playhouse? You got out in fifteen minutes." He lit his cigarette. "It took Hannah an hour when we did it to her." He smiled and blew smoke away from her.

"Then how come she's the one who gets straight As? And everyone thinks she's perfect." Ali put her head in her hands again. Why was she even talking to the kid who used to do all that mean stuff to her, anyway? Because she'd seen him walking around with his shaved head, and she'd known he had the fairies, and she'd asked him to give her some, and now she was stuck with him.

"Any idiot can get straight As," said Michael. "If you want to waste all your time doing homework."

"I don't want to do *any* homework. If I have 'mental acuity' I won't have to," said Ali. That was why she had to do it. Not because of what *might* have happened to Tyler and Molly, or because of some agreement she signed, or so Michael could get his wish. Because she deserved it. She was going to be the smartest kid ever. She lifted her head out of her hands.

"It's going to be fine," said Michael. "I'm going to tell you what I did to get my hair. You don't have to go anywhere near the salon again. We can worry about Mrs. Hopper once your flock is grown."

"Yeah," Ali said. "I can get my wish first." She would still help Mrs. Hopper, just not yet. After all, if she didn't grow her fairies, something bad would happen to *her*, too.

"Cool," Michael said. "Now here's what I did."

"You gave yourself away, Follica!" Grand Miss Coiffure perched on the back of the salon chair, overseeing the floor full of her subjects. She wore a dress made of bright green wrapping paper tied at the waist with a white ribbon. Her bulging, matching green eyes glared at the Mrs. Hopper–shaped fairy. Lockner stood next to the Grand Miss in a wrapping-paper pantsuit (Happy Birthday type), carrying a tiny scroll and pen.

"I was caught in the moment, Miss," said Follica/Mrs. Hopper. "I made a mistake." She kneeled on the ground, her head nearly touching the floor. Other subjects of the Kingdome perched on her back, still with anticipation.

"To think we wasted all those seashells making you big!" the Grand Miss fumed.

"It's not like I asked for it," said Follica. "This body is too hot. It doesn't breathe."

"Silence!" the Grand Miss cried. "Now the children think we can grow big—they don't know that body isn't human, or how hard it was for us to make. What if they refuse to grow our flocks? It takes children to grow us. Children!" She hopped on her chairback, waving her hairpin scepter at the crowd.

"But the wishes, Miss," said Mrs. Hopper. "Surely the wishes—"

"Silence! You will remain silent!" The Grand Miss pointed her scepter at the prostrate woman.

Mrs. Hopper's lips slammed shut. "MM . . . mmmf."

"A fit punishment for overspeaking. Now, the rest of you. Fix this! The girl must not ruin our plans. You will FIX THIS!" She jumped and jumped, waving both her arms this way and that.

"We will, Miss," said Lockner.

"We will, Miss," echoed the crowd.

The bell hanging on the salon door jangled. "Emily! Are you all right?" Ali's mother ran to the old woman kneeling in the middle of the salon floor.

"Mfff." Mrs. Hopper sat up and gave Ali's mother

a wide smile. She clutched her throat and shook her head.

"Oh my," said Ali's mother. "If you're sick, you should go home. I'll call for my appointment later."

Mrs. Hopper nodded and went on smiling.

"Here, let me help you up." Ali's mother lifted the old lady by one arm. "You're light as a feather. Let me take you to a doctor."

Mrs. Hopper shook her head. She pointed to a salon chair and smiled and smiled.

"I can't today," said Ali's mother. "I just wanted to make an appointment. I'll come back later. If you're sure you don't need any help?"

The old lady nodded and smiled, nodded and smiled.

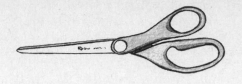

FIVE

Ali looked at the clock. 11:30 P.M. She was cutting it close, but this way, everyone should be asleep. She already had the hair from the drains. It might be enough for all the fairies, but it might not. In case the fairies had already multiplied even more, she wasn't going to be caught off guard. She rolled out of bed, picked up the plastic bag with the hair she'd already collected, grabbed the scissors off her dresser, and listened at her bedroom door. Everything was quiet.

She slipped out into the hallway and tiptoed past the bathroom to Hannah's bedroom. She put her ear against the door, then pushed it open just a crack, so that she was looking at the middle of Hannah's bed. There was Hannah, kissing Deacon. Ugh. She wanted to close the door again, but it was so gross she just couldn't look away.

Hannah ran her hand through Deacon's longish,

blackish hair. How could she stand to touch that mop of grease? "I love your hair," Hannah whispered.

"It was longer," Deacon whispered, running *his* hand through Hannah's hair, "but my brother thought it would be funny to chop it while I was sleeping."

"I think it's perfect," Hannah cooed. They kissed again.

Ali carefully pulled the door shut. So Hannah was out of her mind and out of Ali's grasp for tonight. She'd have to try her mom. Fortunately, her parents slept like a couple of dead logs. Her mother was lying on her stomach, her wavy shoulder-length hair ripe for the taking. Her dad's snores covered Ali's approach as she snuck forward, scissors first. She'd only take a little bit. Her mom would never even notice. Quickly, she snipped off a few locks and stuffed them into her bag.

Something moved on the nightstand next to her mother.

Ali turned her head just in time to see a fairy dodge behind the lamp. She reached out and caught it between two fingers, then ran for the door, shut it behind her, and raced downstairs, trying to be quiet.

"What were you doing up there?" she whispered. The fairy had been so close to her mother's head! "Are there any more of you?"

"Wasn't going to eat. Just going to look." A set of fairy eyes peeked out between the tops of her fingers. Somehow she could tell it was not Pilose.

Ali hurried into the backyard. "You're ungrateful," she huffed. "Look what I'm doing for you. Cutting my own mother's hair off."

"Can't eat off of heads," the fairy whined. "Can only look."

"You can't eat off of heads?"

"Need children to grow us. Need children." The fairy pushed its head farther up, bulging its eyes.

"Then what about Molly Parker?" Ali asked. "What happened to her? Fairies didn't really crawl into her head, did they? But they did something to her." She wasn't going to beat around the bush. These little demons were getting serious. First Mrs. Hopper was a giant fairy, and now this one had been right next to her mom. "And why are the girls wearing these stupid buns and the boys shaving their heads?"

"Cruel, Molly," said the fairy. "Let her hair down. Tortured. Cruelty is not good." It wriggled inside Ali's palm. "It is not good!"

Ali stopped a few feet from the mound. Several fairies stood on top of it in the moonlight, but Ali was too worked up to count them. She shook the fairy in her hand. "Are you saying you can't eat me?

If I let my hair down right now, it will just make you hungry?"

"Against the rules," said the fairy. "You will be punished if you break the rules." It slipped out of Ali's grasp and dropped, unhurt, onto the mound.

"Rules," Ali muttered to herself. "If they really can't eat hair off people's heads, I wonder what else they can't do?" She peered down at the mound. One, two, three . . . six, seven, eight. Eight fairies. She lifted the hair out of the bag with a paper towel and dumped it on top of them. Then she crumpled up the bag and turned toward the house. She shivered. *They are not on me. They are not on me.*

"Hey!"

Ali looked back. There was Michael, climbing over the fence. As he dropped into the dirt a few feet away, there was a crash from the house. Deacon picked himself up off the ground outside Hannah's window and lumbered toward them. Hannah didn't have a tree, but an unstable pile of cinder blocks and firewood sat next to the wall. Deacon must have knocked it over.

"Well, well," Deacon said, not very quietly.

"Shh!" Ali put her finger to her lips.

Deacon grinned and swatted his greasy locks out

of his face. "Guess me and Hannah aren't the only lovebirds." He made kissy noises at Michael while leering sideways at Ali.

"Shut up!" said Michael.

"Gross!" said Ali at the same time.

"I'll leave the back door open," said Deacon. He gave another large lip smack right in Michael's ear, winked at Ali, and jumped over the fence.

Michael looked down at his feet. "Um . . . sorry about my brother," he whispered.

Ali rolled her eyes. "Whatever. I just want to get away from these monsters."

"I wanted to tell you—make sure you read the directions."

"I already read them." Ali glanced down and quickly counted the fairies. If all eight of them were there, they *couldn't* be crawling on her.

"Just—that's all I can say."

"You can't be here!" Pilose jumped on top of the mound, rising above the others, and pointed a tiny finger at Michael.

"I'm just telling her—"

"Go home!" said Pilose.

"Fine. Good night, Ali." Michael wrinkled his nose at the fairies, gave Ali a hard look, and started climbing the fence. He didn't take his eyes off her until he'd dropped down on the other side.

Finally. Ali rushed back into the house and set her alarm for 4:30 a.m. Deacon couldn't *possibly* be in Hannah's room then.

"He wasn't supposed to tell her," said Pilose.

"'Read the directions' is on the approved list," said the second flock starter, whose name was Ringlet. He was holding a scroll, and he peered at it in the moonlight.

"He was trying to tell her more." Pilose sat on the mound. Her belly was already beginning to rumble. Why did she still have to be on flock duty? The others would all be in the Kingdome, feasting to their hearts' content.

"But the rules say—"

"Rules. We follow them, and so must they!" Pilose jumped to her feet and pointed her long finger at Ringlet's nose. "If he tries anything else, he won't get his wish. The Grand Miss will take him the way she took the other two!"

"Should we report this to her?" Ringlet asked, gingerly pushing Pilose's finger out of his face.

"No, no. Let's leave her out of this. We can't have her knowing we let a baby escape into the human house. He let slip even more information than that giant human dunderhead. Thank goodness he didn't say anything about the plan."

"He *is* only a baby," said Ringlet.

"I doubt Bunny—I mean 'the Grand Miss'—would care."

The scroll disappeared into thin air, and the two fairies disappeared into their mound.

SIX

ALI shut her bedroom door behind her and shook her shoulders, even though she knew in her mind that no fairies had gotten on her. The clock said 6:30 a.m. Hannah had slept right through Ali's little snip, and the fairies hadn't given any trouble while she'd fed them. But now there were ten. She'd already had to build another mound. How was she going to manage when they multiplied again? If she took any more hair from Hannah or her mom, they'd start to notice.

Read the directions. She'd been so distracted last night that she'd forgotten what Michael had said. Well, she wasn't going to get any more sleep this morning. She might as well read them again. She sat down at her desk and unfolded the piece of paper. She blinked. This couldn't be right. The paper was completely blank. She turned it over, but there was nothing on the back either. It had to be the right paper. There was the black grease stain in the upper-left-hand corner. Did

Michael know this was going to happen? Why hadn't he just told her?

"Come on, show me the stupid directions," she said out loud.

The paper crinkled all by itself. Suddenly the page was filled with writing. It was in the same childish handwriting as before, but these directions were definitely different.

RULES

You must not let the fairies eat your own hair.

You must not quit growing your flock before
   you have 100 fairies.

You must not help any other child gather hair.

You must not flaunt your delicious hair in
   front of fairies. You must shave your head
   or wear your hair this way:

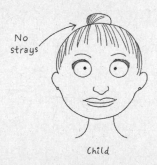

No strays

Child

All hair must be human.

Hmm. She'd been doing these things already, though she didn't understand why she couldn't use her own hair if she wanted to. After all, the fairies thought it was so delicious that it would be cruel for her to wear it down. She flipped the paper over.

CONSEQUENCES

Drastic reduction in body mass.
Slavery.
Increased proportional size of eyes.

What? Was that what had happened to Tyler and Molly? Had they been shrunk and turned into fairy slaves? What if Michael hadn't told her to read the directions again? These evil fairies weren't playing fair. Just as she was about to crumple up the paper in a huff, the drawing of the "child" disappeared, and in its place, a picture of Jennifer Jackson materialized. This was no crude drawing, but a photograph, and it showed Jennifer as she was now—more gorgeous than a movie star. Then the picture suddenly changed, showing Jennifer as she had been. She wasn't exactly ugly, but Ali couldn't deny that the first picture was a whole lot better.

So they really could deliver on their promised

wishes. Was that what they were trying to say? For some reason, Ali had never doubted that. The fairies existed, so magic existed, too. Jennifer's transformation and Natalie Buckmaster's new diva singing voice were just icing on the proverbial cake. Natalie Buckmaster . . . there was someone who wasn't full of shallow nonsense. She was no prettier than Jennifer had been, but she'd chosen an actual talent. Maybe Ali should ask Natalie how she'd made it to one hundred fairies without losing her mind.

Ali crumpled up the directions and tossed the paper at the wall. Slavery. So the fairies had gotten Molly, Tyler, and now Mrs. Hopper. Natalie Buckmaster and Jennifer had gotten their wishes, and so had Jonathan Yeager, who was the biggest bully in school, and Beth Pickler, the girl who was allergic to everything, plus whoever gave them their fairies. Ali didn't know what wishes those kids had picked, but they hadn't disappeared. It was possible to make it through this and get your wish and be done with it, and that was what Ali was going to do.

"What happened to my haaaaaaaair!" Hannah screeched.

Oops.

"Aliiiiiiiiiiiiiiiiiiiiiiiiii!"

Ali sighed. She'd taken less than an inch. Hannah's hair was plenty thick enough to feed all ten fairies with that much.

Ali's door burst open.

Hannah stormed in, holding a lock of hair between her fingers. "You did this, didn't you!" She stomped over to Ali's dresser and picked up the telltale scissors. "Your stupid boyfriend Michael gave you this idea, didn't he?"

"I thought I repelled boys," said Ali, trying not to look at the scissors.

"This is serious, Alison Elizabeth!" Hannah screamed. "It's all uneven! I have to go to Mrs. Hopper's, and *you're* going to pay for it." She slammed down the scissors and picked up Ali's piggy bank. She jerked the stopper out and dumped a wad of bills and change onto the table.

Ali stood up. "Don't go to Mrs. Hopper's!"

"You think I'm going to walk around looking like this?" Hannah counted Ali's bills. "Eight dollars? Agh!" Hannah picked up the scissors, waved them menacingly at Ali, and stormed out of the room again, slamming the door.

"What's going on here?" Ali's mom asked from the hallway.

"She cut my hair off while I was sleeping!" said Hannah.

"Calm down, Hannah," said Ali's mom. "There's more shampoo in the hall closet."

"What?" Hannah screamed. "Aaagh!" Her feet pounded on the staircase.

"A lot of yelling over a little shampoo," said Ali's dad. His footsteps followed Hannah's down.

Shampoo?

Her mom knocked on the door. "Everything okay, honey?" she called.

"Everything's fine," said Ali. But it wasn't true. She stared at the coins scattered across her dresser. Money wasn't going to help Tyler and Molly. What if the fairies were doing something bad to them? They needed help now, not after Ali got her wish. *There must be a way to help Tyler and Molly without breaking any rules,* Ali thought.

SEVEN

ALI pushed Jennifer into the girls' bathroom.

"Hey, the bell just rang." Jennifer tried to slip past Ali, but Ali blocked her path.

"I know. We need to talk."

Jennifer frowned. The crinkles at the edges of her mouth only made her look more beautiful. "If this is about your flock, I can't help you."

"I know. It's not about that. Just come with me, okay?" She grabbed Jennifer's hand and dragged her out of the bathroom and down the hall. At the first door leading outside, she pulled Jennifer onto the sidewalk behind the school building.

Michael and Natalie Buckmaster were waiting there. Natalie stood three feet away from Michael, her arms folded over her chest.

"Hey, ugly," said Michael.

Jennifer rolled her eyes. "Okay, what's going on?"

"Has anyone seen Jonathan Yeager or Beth Pickler?" Ali asked.

"Jonathan?" Jennifer snorted. "Good luck getting *him* to help you."

"I heard he used his wish for a hex," said Natalie. "His own cousin. Made him so ugly you can't look at him without screaming." She snickered.

Yeah, that sounded like Jonathan. He was the only kid in school who was both older and meaner than Michael.

"Then it'll have to be just us," said Ali. "We've got four people."

"Four people for what?" asked Natalie. "What's the big deal?"

"The big deal is that Mrs. Hopper's been replaced by a giant fairy—and Tyler and Molly must have been turned into fairy slaves!" She rushed through the whole story.

"Well, they didn't follow the directions," said Natalie. "They knew what they were getting into."

"Maybe not," Ali said. "I wouldn't have read the part about consequences if Michael hadn't told me to read the directions again. *And* I probably would have tried dog hair. Plus, who deserves to be made into slaves?" She turned to Natalie. "You gave Molly her fairies! You *have* to help her."

"When she didn't finish, I had to find somebody else. Thanks to her, I almost lost my wish!" Natalie's speaking voice sounded just like it always had—screechy. She stalked back into the building without waiting to hear Ali's reply.

"She almost lost her wish? Is that all you guys can think about, too?" Ali demanded.

Jennifer hadn't looked up during Ali's entire story. Now she felt for loose strands around her top-of-the-head bun.

"Michael?"

He rubbed one giant shoe across the sidewalk. "Can't it wait until you grow your flock?"

"Wait?" This was ridiculous. Two kids had been turned into *fairy slaves*. How could they not care? "You guys are the most selfish, chicken, worthless human beings in the United States! So there's a chance you won't get to be a football star? At least you get to be six feet tall!"

"You were going to wait to help Mrs. Hopper," said Michael.

Ali didn't have a good response to that, so she

ignored it. "And you—" She poked a finger in Jennifer's face. "You *got* your wish. What do you have to lose now?"

"I saw her," Jennifer whispered.

"What?" said Michael.

Jennifer looked up. Tears were forming in her perfect, deep blue eyes. "I saw Molly. We were in the park next door to her house. It was getting late, and we were walking back. Her bun was falling out, so she started undoing it. I told her not to. I said, 'Don't let it hang there. Wait until we get inside.' But she kept taking it out." Tears dripped down Jennifer's porcelain cheeks, sparkling like diamonds. "She let it fall down over her shoulders. Her hair was really long. They came out of the grass. They climbed up her legs." She sniffed and wiped her eyes. "They climbed up her back, and then . . . It was so fast. She didn't have time to scream. She was just suddenly gone. Her clothes and everything. She was just gone." She rubbed her hand over the back of her head, checking for stray strands again.

Ali stared at her. "Is that why you're still wearing the bun?"

"I can't take it down," Jennifer sobbed. "I'm scared."

Michael shifted his weight and started scraping

the sidewalk with his other foot. "Well, what do you think we can do about it, anyway?"

"I don't know exactly," said Ali, "but there has to be something. I want my wish as much as you do. We have to think of a way to help them without breaking any rules. What if we tell our parents?"

The door opened next to Ali, and Mr. Johnson, the vice principal, stuck his head out. "You kids need to get to class," he barked.

"It won't work," said Jennifer. She wiped her eyes with one hand. "Mr. Johnson, our friends have been captured by evil fairies who love hair. What should we do?"

"Well, you should have finished the project before class. Now get inside!" He thrust the door open and waved them in.

"See," Jennifer whispered, "we *can't* tell adults about them."

That explained the bit about the shampoo.

"That's why you gave them to *me*, isn't it," said Michael. He loped slowly down the hall behind them, hands in his pockets. "You didn't want any of your *friends* to end up like Molly."

"I'm sorry," Jennifer whispered.

"You better hope I get my wish." Michael turned

around and stomped back toward the door leading outside.

"Wait! Aren't you going to help us stop the fairies?" Ali called after him, but he kicked the door open and barreled through. Where was the Michael who'd cared enough to warn Ali about the directions? She'd thought he cared about Mrs. Hopper, too.

"It's too late for help with your project now," said Mr. Johnson, waving both girls along. "Let's get you two to class."

"Only four shells?" Lockner swatted the girl-slave with his scroll.

"I'm so hungry," said Molly. The pile of shells reached halfway to the top of Mrs. Hopper's coat closet.

Tyler heaved his weight against the mousse bottle, sending a spray of white goop into the scrap of cloth that Molly was holding in front of her like a sheet. The force of the spray nearly toppled her over.

"You'll have your hair when you've encrusted your ten shells," said Lockner. "You!" He pointed to Tyler. "Chop chop!"

"Why do we have to do this?" asked Tyler. "Isn't mousse supposed to go in girls' hair?"

"Hair products enhance power," said Lockner. He rolled his eyes. These children were so ignorant. But their shameful lack of education would come in handy. They'd never guess what the mousse and the shells were for. He smiled to himself.

Tyler picked up one end of the cloth, and the two slaves lugged it over to the next shell, the remains of a particularly large sea snail.

Lockner waited until Molly and Tyler had unloaded the contents of the cloth onto the shell, then slid haughtily under the closet door.

"Hair," said Molly.

"Hair," said Tyler.

EIGHT

I'll give you some hair," said Crista. She was choking Teddy Tux almost as hard as Michael had.

"No, that's not what I meant. I can get it some other way." Ali was sitting at her desk, nervously fingering the direction sheet. It was blank again.

"It'll be fine," said Crista. "It grows back."

Crista did have nice long hair. It wasn't too thick, but it would still feed a fair number of fairies. Ali shook her head. "I don't know."

The door burst open, and Hannah stalked into the room. Her hair was a good six inches shorter than before. "Look!" she squealed. "I asked Mrs. Hopper for a little trim and she did this!" Hannah stopped mid-rant and glared at Crista. "We'll talk about this *later*." She turned and stomped out, slamming the door behind her.

Ali sighed. At least "Mrs. Hopper" hadn't taken *Hannah*.

"See? You can't take it from her again," Crista observed.

"I know, but it's not fair. I wish you could get something out of it. I'll still pass them on to you if you want them."

"*If I want them?* Ali, are you serious? You can't pass them on to anyone! You just have to finish growing your flock and get out of this."

"But the agreement says I have to pass them on," said Ali. *And after all this, I deserve to get my wish,* she thought. But she knew better than to say that to Crista.

There was a knock on the closed window.

"What's that?" Crista set Teddy down and walked over to the window. Her long, straight brown hair swooshed back and forth as she walked. It really was fine, beautiful hair, and the color was deep and pure, not muddled and mousy like Ali's.

Crista peered out. "Is someone out there?"

"It's probably Michael," said Ali. "I don't know why he can't *call*. Just open it."

Crista pushed the window open as far as it would go and stepped back toward the bed.

Branches rustled, there was a loud crack, and a boy fell into the room. It was definitely not Michael.

Michael's large frame would have made a much louder crash.

"Oof," said the boy into the carpet.

"Who the heck are you?" Ali asked. She and Crista each took one of his arms and helped him up.

He brushed himself off, sending dirt and twigs floating down. Then he looked straight at them.

"Oh my—" Crista put her hand over her mouth and turned away.

Ali wanted to do the same, but she held herself back. The boy standing in front of them was absolutely the ugliest person she'd ever seen in her entire life. His nose was bulbous, and not just because it was so unthinkably large. It also housed the largest of the many zits that spread out across his face and down his neck. His eyes were crooked, his chin was lopsided, his cheeks were wrinkled, and his hair was thin and wispy, barely covering the flakes that dislodged from his head as he finished brushing the dirt off. Ali didn't think she'd ever seen him before, but she knew that this level of ugliness wasn't just an unfortunate combination of bad genes. This boy was the victim of a hex.

"You can tell, can't you?" said the boy. "I never used to look like this—but no one else remembers. Please, you have to help me!"

Crista had managed to turn back around, and she cautiously removed her hand from her mouth. "What's wrong with you?"

"It was Jonathan Yeager. Do you know him? He's my cousin," the boy said. "He's in eighth grade. Anyway, he hates me for no reason, and he had me hexed! I saw you with your bun and I thought, that girl knows what's going on. That girl can tell me how to get my own fairies so I can get my face back!"

"So *you're* Jonathan Yeager's cousin," Ali said. "I've heard about you. You don't go to our school, do you?"

"No, I live in Harrisburg," said the boy. "My name's Jared." Harrisburg was a tiny town about ten miles away.

"Well, Jared," said Ali, "I do need someone to give my fairies to, but it's dangerous." She told Jared about Mrs. Hopper and Tyler and Molly.

"I don't care about any of that," said Jared. "*Look* at me!"

"Can you even undo a hex?" asked Crista. "I bet you can't."

"Well, the list didn't say anything about that," said Ali. "They have to put it in the rules." She picked up the piece of paper again and flipped it over to the side with the grease stain. The last time she had asked for the directions, writing had appeared on the paper. So why wouldn't it work again? "Can you undo a hex against yourself or not?" she asked.

You must never tell any other child the contents of the directions.

YOU MAY SAY:
Read the directions.
Follow the directions.
Beware the directions.

"Well, what does it say?" asked Jared.
"Nothing," said Ali. She flipped the paper over.

Improvements may include I'm-rubber-you're-glue-bounce-off-me-and-stick-to-you-unhex-hex-backsies.

Anyone who would cast a hex deserves one.

The directions had answered Ali's specific question. Interesting. But if she couldn't tell Jared what the contents were, how was she supposed to tell him that he could get himself unhexed?

"Well?" asked Jared.

"You can have my fairies," said Ali. "If you really don't want them?" She raised her eyebrows at Crista.

"You can't be for real." Crista grabbed the pair of child's scissors that Ali had rescued from her old school supplies. The scissors had been sitting on Ali's pillow, waiting for her next foray into Hannah's room. Crista pulled her hair around and began hacking off the bottom several inches.

"Crista, don't," said Ali.

"No, I don't want the stupid fairies." She kept cutting. "What kind of fairies hurt people like this? They're not fairies, they're little demons."

"Oh, come on," said Ali. She'd thought that, too, but she wasn't going to say it out loud. "Demons don't exist."

"If fairies can exist, anything can," said Jared. He scratched his bulbous nose.

Crista finished cutting, leaving her hair in a pile on the bed. It had been long enough that it didn't look so different now. "One minute you want to save Tyler and Molly and poor old Mrs. Hopper, and the next you're talking about passing the fairies on, so there'll be even more fairies. Don't you see how ridiculous that is?"

"He wants them," said Ali. "Look at what Jonathan Yeager did to his face."

"It's not just my face," said Jared.

Crista's eyes opened wide, bulging almost like a fairy's. "You're lucky that's all that happened to you! They have all these rules that are trying to trick you. You'll end up as slaves or even worse. But neither of you cares what I think." She pointed at Ali. "All you want is to be smart? Well, you need it! Maybe you *should* pass your fairies on. Maybe when you're this big *genius* you can figure out a way to clean up this whole *mess!*" She stormed out of the room, slamming the door exactly like Hannah had.

"She's probably right," said Jared, "but I can't live like this. My *mom* won't even look at me."

"I know," said Ali. Crista was just trying to protect her. She'd given up all that hair. But she had to pass her fairies on, or Ali herself would end up a slave. And now this poor, hideous kid had come begging for help. By passing her fairies on, she'd be doing him a favor. "Write your phone number down." She handed Jared her school notebook. "I'll call you as soon as my flock is ready."

"Oh, thank you! Thank you so much. I'll pay you

back somehow. I'll help you with those other people as soon as I have my looks back."

"You could help us now," Ali said. "I'm trying to think of a way to rescue them and still get our wishes."

"No way," said Jared. "I'm not getting on those fairies' bad side!" With that, he gave her a big, hideously ugly smile and climbed back out the window.

Great, Ali thought. *He's probably just as bad as Jonathan Yeager.* After all, you couldn't be hexed unless you deserved it. But she'd worry about Jared later. Right now, she had to think of a plan. She picked up the directions again.

"How can I save Tyler and Molly?" she asked.

"That was lovely hair, Pilose," said Ringlet. They were sitting at the bottom of their second mound, having just made sure that all nineteen of their charges were safely asleep.

"Hmm." Pilose watched the silent human house. She wished she were inside, not out here in the cold and dirt.

"Oh, come on," said Ringlet. "It won't be long now. All this discomfort will be worth it."

"You think Bunny won't come up with some other way to make us miserable, once she's gotten what she wants?"

"Maybe," said Ringlet, "but think about it! We'll be the ones in that big house, sleeping in those nice warm beds, eating all sorts of yummy food. They'll be the ones out here in the cold."

"We wouldn't have to eat hair at all if Bunny hadn't botched that un-enslavement spell," said Pilose, wrapping her arms around her bony knees. "'A child's *hair*,' the directions said. Not a whole entire ponytail."

"Well, would you rather still be a slave to the behavior of dirty little human children?"

"What are we now?" said Pilose. "Sitting here waiting until that urchin feeds us again. Yes, we complained about our lives as Divvy-imps. I complained as much as the next imp. Who wanted to be tied to children, being forced to reward them when they were good and punish them only when they were bad? But that was nature's way, Ringlet. Children needed us to keep the balance, to divvy out life's just deserts. And in exchange, we got to live inside with them, where it was warm. We had as much as we wanted to eat, and we never had to eat a strand of hair. We may have had to reward them for being good, but we got to dole out some nice punishments, too, didn't we? The punishments made it worth it."

"Hmm, there were some good ones," said Ringlet.

"Remember when Hannah pulled Alison's hair in a fight over a stuffed toy?" asked Pilose.

64

Ringlet chuckled. "We put some good knots in her hair after her next bath, didn't we?"

"And when Alison hid Hannah's favorite shoes until Hannah cried like a hyena?"

"Ah," said Ringlet. "A nice, fat stubbed toe." Both fairies smiled at the memory of Ali's pain.

"See?" said Pilose. "There were some good times."

"A stubbed toe, a bad hair day, a headache. It was all right, but it was minor magic," said Ringlet. "Bunny can make us all big. Not like Follica, but real."

"Big," said Pilose. "I can think of better things to do with all that power."

NINE

HOW TO RE-SIZE A REDUCED CHILD:

(1) Combine:

　　One full-sized human

　　One full can hairspray

(2) Mix ingredients in presence of child to be re-sized.

One full - sized human

You must be this tall to qualify

Sorry, not tall enough!

Eat more veggies!

(3) Apply magic of 10 un-enslaved Divvy-imps.

Un-enslaved Divvy-imps? What on earth were they? Just as Ali was wondering, the entire (3) line disappeared and was replaced by:

Forget you saw that.

Which was replaced by:

(3) Apply magic of 10 fairies.

Hmm. Did that mean fairies and Divvy-imps were the same thing? And was Ali not supposed to know? If so, there had to be some way she could use it. Maybe Divvy-imps had some weakness, something Ali should know or could find out. She would have to think about that. But there was another issue. What would happen to the "full-sized human"? She didn't want that person getting turned into a fairy slave. Unless, of course, the "full-sized human" was someone who deserved it.

What if she used Jonathan Yeager? That would be in the spirit of the directions about the hex. If anyone deserved to be turned into a fairy—or a Divvy-imp—it was the kid who'd done a hex himself. Still, there had to be a way that didn't involve putting someone else in danger. And how was she supposed to get ten fairies to use their magic anyway?

Wait a minute, Ali thought. *I've got a whole bunch of fairies right here in the backyard who need me to feed them hair.* All she needed to do was rescue Tyler and Molly, and then she could force Pilose and the others to help them. And Ali knew exactly where Tyler and Molly must be—the "Kingdome," also known as Mrs. Hopper's hair salon.

She slammed the paper down on the desk and picked up the phone.

"Hello?"

"Michael? It's Ali."

"Oh."

"'Oh'? Don't 'Oh' me. I'm calling because you have to help me. Tyler was your friend, wasn't he?"

"Not really."

"Come on. Tomorrow we're going to get Jennifer and anyone else who can help, and we're going over to Mrs. Hopper's hair salon. At least we can take back Tyler and Molly, and then if we want to make them big, the directions said—"

"Don't tell me!"

Ali cringed. "Right. So I'm going out to feed my fairies before school tomorrow. Meet me out there." She slammed the phone down before he had a chance to say no. She didn't have time to listen to him argue. She had a few more calls to make.

Meanwhile, at the Kingdome, the Divvy-imps (for that is what they still were, un-enslaved or not) were taking full advantage of their newfound freedom to have something they had always wanted—something they had been forced to watch children having for generation after generation, but that they could never have themselves. The imps were having a birthday party.

"And many more!

On hairy shore!

And hair for you!

For all you do!

HAPPY BIRTHDAY!"

The imps cheered.

Bunny bowed to the crowd from her perch on top of the salon chair, rustling her wrapping-paper dress. "Thank you, thank you! I'm so proud to celebrate another week as your Grand Miss Coiffure. Let the slumber party begin!"

Chattering noisily, the imps began dragging their beds out of the nooks and crannies where they'd been hidden for the day. Since the imps were super-strong for their size, this didn't present too much trouble. In a few minutes, they had rows of bunk beds assembled on the salon floor. In Mrs. Hopper's giant fake body,

Follica watched the proceedings sullenly, wishing she could join the party. She would have to sleep upstairs in the real Mrs. Hopper's apartment. It was all right, but it was very adult and not much fun.

"One, two, three!" cried Bunny. She raised her scepter and the rest of the imps raised their arms, and the bunk beds, which had been quite ordinary and sparse, were now covered with high canopies, light and silky and brightly colored. Orange streamers ran between the beds, and balloons the size of salt shakers rose above the imps' heads.

Follica carried a bag of hair clippings to the center of the room, where the imps had left a large space. *I've scrambled all over town to scrape up these clippings,* Follica thought, *and all without being able to talk. Not that they'd care to notice.* She dumped the hair into the empty space.

"And now for some cake!" cried Bunny, and the imps jumped into the pile as one, sending clippings floating into the air in an exuberant cloud.

Later that night, when the imps were full of hair and sleeping peacefully, Bunny leaned over the edge of her top bunk (which was just a little bit higher than everyone else's top bunk) and whispered, "Lockner. Are you awake?"

"Yes, Miss," said Lockner sleepily. Whenever Bunny wished to talk, which was often, he was awake.

"Do you remember our first birthday party?"

"Yes, Miss," said Lockner.

"It was everything I'd dreamed of," said Bunny. "Worth all the travel and trial and tears it took to find the Eternal Imp and the *Great Book*."

Lockner rolled over. It was a good story, but he had already heard it many times. "Mmm-hmm," he said.

"I was so sick of that perfect little girl, Virginia, I would have done it even if it cost me my magic." Bunny leaned back on her pillow. "How could the fates be so cruel as to tie a great, noble imp like me to that disgusting creature?"

"What was so bad about her, Miss?" asked Lockner for the thousandth time.

"Lockner, there was never a child who was more good. Day after day after day, little Virginia ate all her vegetables, did all her homework, and never talked back. She never threw a tantrum or said a mean word to anyone. She was as generous as a saint and as pretty as a being with tiny eyes can be. I had to dole out reward after reward to the sweet little angel. I saved her from nasty falls, sweetened her boring healthy cereal, and made her mother forget to limit her TV. And that wasn't all! The urchin was so good that I was forced to give extreme rewards. I had to grant her even greater beauty, prodigious musical talent, and the starring role in her school play."

"She must have done *something* bad," said Lockner.

"Aha, you'd think so! But no. One time I was sure I was finally going to be able to punish her. Another child flew into a rage and slapped Virginia in the face. But what did that little saint do? She hugged the other child and said, 'I'm so sorry you're upset. Would you like some ice cream?' That was the last straw! I knew I couldn't live that way another minute."

"Oh my goodness," said Lockner. Even after many tellings, this part of the story never failed to make him shiver. A life with no punishments? How horrible! No wonder Bunny had been the one to help them break their unfair ties to children.

"So I thought about the old stories," said Bunny. "I remembered the legend of Impoliptus, the one we all learned from our flock starters at an early age. A long time ago, before our flock starters and their flock starters lived," Bunny began. As she spoke, Lockner mouthed the words. When he had first heard the ancient legend, he had never imagined that it was really true. "Divvy-imps were not Divvy-imps yet," Bunny continued. "Our ancestors were wild imps, living off the land and not tied to the humans. These wild imps lived by the ocean to the west of here. They fished and scavenged for edible plants, but that work was quick. The rest of their days they spent frolicking. They swam in the salt water, tormented sea creatures, or sunned themselves on the sweet sand.

"They were happy like this, never knowing any different. But one day an imp came walking out of the forest. This imp, whose name was Impoliptus, carried with him a giant book. It covered his whole back, and he was doubled over as he walked. At this time, no one had seen an imp from the outside before. They had not even known that other imps existed.

"Impoliptus took the book from his back and set it on top of a great rock. And when he stood up straight, he stood a full inch above the other imps. 'I have great wisdom to impart,' said Impoliptus. And he proceeded to read from the *Great Book of the Imps,* which explained that imps were truly capable of powerful magic. The imps could have control over the humans, who were encroaching on their pristine beaches. They did not have to live in the open, but could live in the great houses the humans built. They could eat roast beef instead of tiny sea creatures and grasses.

"Now, the imps didn't know what roast beef was, of course, but Impoliptus described it as a great delicacy, which, as we know, was no lie. All the imps needed to do to obtain this great power, said Impoliptus, was to voluntarily participate in the ceremony described in the *Great Book*. And the imps, so the story goes, were astounded and honored by the reward they were offered, and they performed the ritual with hearts full of gladness."

"Some are naughty, some are nice," Lockner whispered.

"Yes," said Bunny. "Impoliptus produced a sack full of human fingernail clippings, and he placed a clipping on each imp's head. Nail clippings are similar to hair, you see—they contain the essence of human power. The imps climbed into a pyramid, with Impoliptus on the very top, holding the *Great Book*, and they chanted:

> "Some are naughty
>
> Some are nice
>
> Some are almost six feet high
>
> Most are mixture
>
> Good and bad
>
> Most need coal as well as pie
>
> Most need fun with their black eyes!
>
> Children!
>
> We live for children!
>
> Children!
>
> They come from children!"

"The imps clutched their nail-clipping headdresses and jumped as one out of their pyramid. When they hit the sand beneath them,

Impoliptus was gone, and the book along with him. All that was left of him was a long arrow in the sand, pointing away from the ocean, toward the imps' new homes, toward their new lives of great magic."

The two imps lay in silence for a minute, contemplating the story. What did it mean, that they had once been free? Had Impoliptus tricked their ancestors into giving up their freedom, or had he given them the beginnings of something great? Were they now on the right track, on their way to complete un-enslavement?

"So what did you do, Miss?" Lockner asked. Now that he was fully awake, he was lost in the story, imagining that it was he who had gone on Bunny's journey, he who had found the great Impoliptus.

"There was another part to the legend," said Bunny. "A part that one of my flock starters told me in secret, after the other imps had gone to bed. He knew I was destined for greatness, you see. He said that after Impoliptus had completed his revered work of binding the imps to their great magic—and to children—he retired to a cave 'where sky meets sea.' And that was all my flock starter could tell me. No one knew where this cave was. But I knew I could find it. I had to! I would read the *Great Book of the Imps*, and I would find the spell that would reverse the magic and set the imps free from children once and for all!"

"How did you find it?" Lockner whispered.

"I thought about it and thought about it," Bunny said. "Until

I almost despaired. I had no idea where the ocean was. No imp had returned to the sea since the time of the Enslavement. But I listened to my family. I paid attention to every detail of every conversation, every word written and read in that house. And finally it came. 'Let's go to the coast for the weekend,' said Virginia's mother, just like that.

"So that Saturday morning, they all piled into the car— Virginia, her mother and father, and their dog, Boot. Oh, that dog was a hairy mess. Those perfect people couldn't be troubled to give him a bath, could they? And of course, dogs can see us half the time. It took two long, miserable hours. That dog chased me around the backseat, dripping hair and spit. Once, I jumped into the front seat, but Boot jumped after me and nearly caused an accident. I don't need to tell you what would have happened to me if the little princess had bought it. That would have been the end of me too. So I had to suffer in the backseat, being chased and drooled on, listening to Virginia laughing every time Boot jumped.

"Once they finally stopped the car, I had no easy task. I didn't know where on the human maps the old imp homeland was. I risked great danger separating from my child. It was unheard of, unimagined, the riskiest separation ever undertaken by a modern imp. With only my memory of the stories told by my flock starters to guide me, I began walking the vast, untamed shoreline."

Lockner imagined himself walking the shoreline, felt the pains of separation.

"It took all day and all night," Bunny went on. "I had to draw on magic I'd never known I could use for my own purposes. Dig deep into the fabric of my inner strength. And then, all of a sudden, I knew where I was. There were the dunes our flock starters had sung about."

Lockner didn't remember any singing, but he remembered the stories about the old frolicking days of free impdom. He let out a small sigh.

"I felt our ancestors in the air. This was where they'd swum in the water and sunned themselves on the beach. Though I have to say, it was a little cold for that. The Great Impoliptus, or at least his *Great Book of the Imps*, had to be around there somewhere. I just needed to find this place 'where sky meets sea.' It sounded so simple that I wondered what the big mystery was all about. I walked down to the water and looked around. There was the sky and there was the sea. But no one was there except a pesky crab that tried to poke me with its unsanitary claw. I walked up and down the beach, calling out 'Great Imp! Great Imp!' like a crazy imp, until night began to fall again and I sat down in the receding water, utterly exhausted.

"You cannot imagine my feelings then, Lockner. Separated from my child, feeling the pains that accompany rewards not given—as if ants were eating my arms off."

She wasn't exaggerating. Rewards not given were the worst. Punishments not doled out only caused a little tickle.

"It began to rain then. I was exhausted and already soaking wet and in pain. I had to find somewhere to rest before heading back to find Virginia. I dragged myself away from the ocean toward a pile of boulders near the cliff edge. I hoped that being small, I might find a nook or cranny where I could wait out the rain.

"It was a long wet slog, and I was almost ready to drop into the sand and be buried in it, when I heard a female imp voice. 'See!' the imp cried. 'See! See!'

"'Hello!' I shouted back. My voice must have been barely audible, I was so tired and thirsty. But an imp appeared from behind a rock. 'See!' she called, and she waved me forward. The sight of this welcoming imp, with her lovely seaweed dress and flowing imp hair, buoyed my spirits just enough. I pressed forward and climbed up the last hill of sand, until I was standing before her. She was a vision, Lockner. A veritable angel of impness.

"'Come with me,' said this angel. And I followed her over a miraculously dry path through the rocks to a cave. It was a warm, dry space hidden from outside view by an overhang. The entrance was only wide enough for a single imp to pass through, but inside, the cave was large and majestic, not like a cave at all. It was furnished like a human house, with thick white carpet (perfectly clean, mind you), a lovely living-room set, and a full-sized bunk bed. Three imps could have slept on either of these wonderful mattresses, yet these two imps apparently each had one for themselves.

"Yes, there were two imps, for now that I was inside, I saw a male imp standing in front of those very beds, watching me with a solemnity and grace that I knew could mean only one thing: this was Impoliptus, the Great Imp of the stories. I knew then and there that the stories were all true."

Lockner listened, rapt. The Great Imp, Impoliptus himself! If only he could have been there.

"The Great Imp's hair reached below his chin, and it was thick and black, yet it never blocked a micron of his face as he walked forward to meet me. 'You are Bunniumpton,' he said. 'I have been waiting for you to come.' I was speechless for a moment, staring at him. I couldn't believe that he had said my name, my *full* name, as if he knew me. 'Is this where sky meets sea?' I asked. 'It is where Sky shouts, "See!"' said the Great Imp solemnly. 'Perhaps the imps did not hear me quite right in their hurry to embrace their new lives. This is my sister, Sky. Each night she goes to the edge of the rocks and shouts, in case any of our flock have chosen to return to us.' The female imp bowed slightly to me and smiled. 'Have a seat,' she said, 'and we will talk.'

"We talked all night, Lockner. The Great Imp warned me never to repeat what was said then. But when the morning broke, he brought the *Great Book of the Imps* out of thin air, and with great ceremony, he gave it to me. 'It is time for the next chapter of the Story of the Imps,' he said. 'The imps have grown past their ties to children. They deserve all the birthday parties and toys that children have. Go and perform the un-enslavement ritual, Bunniumpton. You shall be the Grand Miss of the Flock. Go forth and take your place at the head of this great leap forward for Impkind.'

"So I thanked the Great Imp and went to meet Virginia and her parents. I gave Virginia her weekend's worth of rewards, knowing that my enslavement would soon be over. And here we are, celebrating a birthday party any time we want!"

Always for the Grand Miss and never for us, thought Lockner. Still, it was nice to be done with handing out rewards to children. Even the worst children were sweet sometimes, and he'd certainly had enough of that. If only they weren't stuck with this business of the hair. He rubbed his bald head. He'd had luscious locks himself, once. His head would have rivaled the Great Imp's before the ritual. He sighed. Life was such a sacrifice, even now.

"Goodnight, Lockner," said the Grand Miss.

"Goodnight, Miss," said Lockner. "Happy birthday."

Bunny said nothing. She was remembering the solemn words of the Great Imp. *The magical universe is governed by many rules, Bunniumpton. Some are easy to follow and some are hard. Some make sense and some make little. But you must follow them. They are the rules that created us and keep us strong. If you do not follow the rules, neither I nor the Great Book nor all the imps, fairies, and other sprites combined can protect you from your folly.* "I understand, Great Imp," Bunny had said. "I have always followed the rules."

Bunny rolled over onto her side. There was only a little light from the street, but she could see all her imps lying peacefully in their bunk beds. Soon, they would have houses of their own and real beds. And roast beef and ham and mashed potatoes and strawberries. Soon they would be ready for the Replacement, the spell that would make the imps big once and for all.

TEN

"More," a baby fairy whined.

"I don't have any more. I just brought you lots of nice hair." She'd given them a little bit of Crista's hair that was left over from last night, plus some of her mother's, plus everything she'd collected from the drains at home *and* in the school locker room.

"More."

"There are twenty-five of us now," said Pilose. Her long fingers spread over the baby's chest, holding him back. The other twenty-three fairies poked their heads out of the three mounds.

"Well, I have to think of a way to get more," said Ali. "It doesn't help that I can't use my own. Why is that, anyway?"

"You are our child," said Pilose.

"That still doesn't explain—" Ali stopped as she saw Michael's eyes peering over the fence. "I have to go to school now. You've had plenty of hair for this morning. I'll get you some more this afternoon, okay? Way before midnight." She picked up her backpack from the ground and slung it over one shoulder.

"Soon," said Pilose.

"Hair."

"Hair."

"Hair."

Ali rushed out of the yard and onto the sidewalk, where Michael was waiting. Even though she couldn't hear them anymore, she still felt the word. *Hair.* She had to figure something out before afternoon, but that wasn't her first priority right now.

"Ooh, look who's with his girlfriend again," said Deacon, pushing past Michael and nearly knocking Ali over.

"Hey, watch it," Ali said.

"Deeeeacon!" Hannah trilled from behind Ali. She threw her dainty arms around Deacon's bulky body.

Ali rolled her eyes.

"Come on, goober," said Deacon. "You're gonna get expelled if you miss any more days." He punched Michael on the arm as he walked past them holding Hannah's hand.

"I have to help Ali rescue a couple kids from some evil fairies first," said Michael. "I'll write up an excuse later."

"If you skip school, I'm telling Mom," said Hannah. She ran her hand through her hair and glared at Ali.

"I think your hair looks great short," said Deacon.

"They didn't hear a word about the fairies, did they?" Ali asked, watching them walk away obliviously.

"Not a word," said Michael. "Wish we knew what they *did* hear."

Quiet footsteps sounded behind Ali. She turned around.

"Hi," said Jennifer.

She was trailed by Crista. The two of them had never liked each other, and it didn't look like they were going to start now. Crista stayed a good three feet back.

"Crista, no, you can't help. You've done enough already," Ali said.

"I can't just sit around and wait to find out what happens to you." She flipped her uneven but still long hair. "What if you never come back?"

"Is anyone else coming?" asked Jennifer.

"I called Natalie Buckmaster and Jonathan Yeager, but *they* wouldn't help," said Ali. "Then I called Beth

Pickler—you know, the girl with all the allergies? But she acted like I was trying to sell her Girl Scout cookies. She can't really have forgotten. I mean, she's still in eighth grade."

"She's just chicken," said Jennifer. "She wished for invincibility, but the fairies said that was too greedy, and they threatened her with a greed-hex. I don't know what that is, but she changed her wish to improvement in health. Now she's not allergic to anything. She could probably eat rat poison if she wanted to."

"Well, Beth gave her fairies to you, right, Jennifer? But I don't know who gave them to Natalie or who she gave them to after Molly, or who gave Jonathan his."

"Maybe we should find out," said Michael.

"No! We're not letting another day go by without at least trying to rescue Tyler and Molly."

"Ali's right," said Crista. "We can't let them be fairy slaves."

"Okay, let's get your hair up in the bun just in case," said Ali. "Then we'll go over to Mrs. Hopper's and get Molly and Tyler back."

Ali, Crista, Jennifer, and Michael squatted behind the dumpster in back of Mrs. Hopper's hair salon.

"What now?" whispered Jennifer.

Michael was having the hardest time hiding. He was so big he practically had to curl into a ball. He jumped up, peered into the dumpster, and then curled up again. "All clear, no fairies," he whispered.

"There's no point in sitting out here," said Ali. "I say we just go in there and follow the plan. Michael is going to take some fairies hostage. I'm going to demand Molly and Tyler back. Jennifer and Crista, you stand there looking menacing, like you're ready to stomp on them or something. And if that doesn't work, we go for plan B. You know what to do if that happens, right, Michael?" She hoped that by telling him what to do, she technically wasn't telling him what the directions said.

Michael nodded.

"Okay. They may have magic, but they have rules they have to follow. They need kids to multiply themselves. I bet they can't really do anything to us unless we break the rules, which we haven't. I checked everything, and there's nothing that says we can't take our friends back."

"Are you sure?" asked Crista.

"I'm sure," said Ali. "There were even directions on how to resize someone. Why would they tell us how to do something that was against the rules?"

Michael and Jennifer exchanged a glance while Crista rolled her eyes and shook her head.

"I'll go first," Ali snapped. She stood up and headed for the door, but Michael jumped in front of her and got there first.

He barreled through the door. "Where are you, you little devils?"

Ali pushed in behind him. The hair salon appeared completely empty. "Come on, fake Mrs. Hopper. We know you're all here." *Please don't dump hair on me again. Please don't dump hair on me again.*

Fairy heads popped out from behind the chair backs. Eye upon bulging eye watched them. Tiny voices whispered, too quietly for Ali to understand.

Mrs. Hopper stepped out of a closet to Ali's right, calmly surveying the four of them. What had she been doing in there? She didn't seem at all unnerved.

A fairy dressed in wrapping paper appeared on Mrs. Hopper's shoulder. "You must find your own hair," said the tiny man.

"We're not here for the hair," said Ali. "We're here for our friends Molly and Tyler. We know you turned them into fairy slaves, and we want you to give them back to us."

Ali didn't have to look to know that the fairies were

dropping down from their places on the chairs. They were crowding around the humans.

The door clanged.

Ali looked back. Crista was gone. Jennifer stood with her back to the door, ready to run. So much for being menacing. But Ali wasn't going to back down.

"Where are they?" she demanded.

"Give them back," said Michael. His voice was so quiet, it was almost a whisper. Apparently he'd used up all his courage bursting in front of her. He looked like he was about to run too. Well, let him. She just needed him to do one little thing first. The fairies that crowded silently around their feet weren't going to help, and there was no way she'd be able to pick out which ones were Tyler and Molly. She'd just have to hope her plan worked.

"Now!" she yelled.

Michael bent down and scooped up the fairies nearest to him. He got six of them in one swoop, and they writhed and squirmed in his hand.

"Agh! What's that stink?"

"Cigarettes. Gak!"

"Unholy beast!" All of the fairies in Michael's hand began to cough dramatically. They flailed their arms as if they were drowning.

"Give us Molly and Tyler," said Ali. "Or we're taking your friends."

"Ali!" a voice squeaked. Ali looked down and saw two fairies jumping and waving their arms. Two fairies with hair on their heads!

"Molly, is that you?"

A fairy poked Molly in the back, and she stumbled forward.

"Yes, it's me. We're all right, but they're making us coat seashells with mousse. They're getting ready for some kind of—*mfff.*" A fairy wearing bright red paper clapped a hand over Molly's mouth. Tiny Tyler tried to land a punch on the first fairy, but another fairy restrained him.

Ali kneeled down and held out a hand. "Now just let them walk onto my hand, and we'll leave. We came to take them back, not to hurt anyone."

"Yeah, we don't want to hurt anyone," said Michael, shaking the fairies.

"Fiend!"

"Monster!" The six fairies in Michael's hand wailed. Hot tears dripped from their giant eyes onto Michael's palm.

"Oh, come on," said Michael. "I just gave you a little shake."

"No one is letting anyone go," said a loud, imperious fairy

voice. She stood on the back of one of the salon chairs, and she was wearing a dress made of green wrapping paper and holding a hairpin. "I am Bunniumpton, Grand Miss Coiffure, monarch of the Kingdome of Fairies, and I—"

"You're no fairy!" Ali cried. "You're just a Divvy-imp!"

"What?" Bunny exclaimed. "I am—"

"You're not," said Ali. "I saw it in the directions. It said that to resize a reduced child you had to take one full-sized human—"

"Ali, don't tell us!" Jennifer cried.

"—and one can of hairspray, and the magic of ten un-enslaved Divvy-imps! And then they tried to say I should just forget it but I'm not going to!" Ali had no idea what was so bad about being an imp instead of a fairy, but they never would have said they were fairies if it didn't mean something.

"Once we freed ourselves from children, we cast off our old titles!" Bunny cried. "We demand to be treated as equal sprites! We will call ourselves fairies if we so choose. And we will not be giving any slave children back—children who broke the rules and are only receiving their just deserts." Bunny waved her hairpin, and fairies closed in around Molly and Tyler. One of them gave Ali's hand a good kick.

"Hey!" Ali pulled her hand back. She glanced at Michael.

Michael gulped and nodded.

"Then we'll just have to do what we can right here," Ali said, standing up again.

Michael reached down with his other hand and scooped up four more fairies.

At the same time, Ali pulled a can of hairspray out of her jacket pocket. That was when she realized what was missing from her plan. They hadn't decided who would be the "full-sized" human. It couldn't be Michael—he was in charge of holding the fairies. Jennifer shook her head vigorously and shrank against the door, eyes wide. Ali couldn't spray Jennifer when she was so scared. She couldn't spray anyone she cared about because she had no idea what was going to happen. *I hope Mrs. Hopper counts,* she thought, and she leaped toward Mrs. Hopper and sprayed.

"Mmmf! MMM!" Mrs. Hopper fell back against the closet door.

Ali advanced on her, pushing as hard as she could on the trigger, letting the whole can go in Mrs. Hopper's face.

"You do it," Michael said, shaking the fairies in his fists. "You change them back."

"You can't force a fairy's magic," said one.

The hairspray can sputtered out.

"Do it," said Michael, still shaking the fairies.

"Stink!"

"We'll never . . . gak . . . help you!"

"Monster!" The fairies wailed and wailed.

Mrs. Hopper grabbed the bottle out of Ali's hand and tossed it toward the front of the shop. She was about a foot taller than Ali, and her blue eyes were strangely empty as she advanced. The hairspray covering her face, head, and chest didn't seem to impede her breathing. The sticky film just sat there, obscuring her blank features as she reached for Ali.

"It's not working! Let's go!" Jennifer yelled. "Aaah! Get off me! Get off me!" Jennifer stumbled toward Michael and Ali. Her dress ruffled with the movement of the fairies as they crawled up her stomach and began crawling out of her neckline. "Ali, help! Michael! Get them off me!" Her sentence ended in a squeak.

Please don't let that squeak mean . . . Ali turned her head just enough to see that Jennifer was gone—or at least not big enough for her to see. "Run!" she cried, racing for the door, but Mrs. Hopper's large arm squeezed her neck. The arm was rubbery and twisted around Ali. It wasn't like a real human arm at all.

A great commotion arose from the Kingdome. The fairies screamed and jumped about. Mrs. Hopper let go of Ali. Ali turned and saw Tyler, now as large as he had ever been, holding Mrs. Hopper around the waist.

"Are you all right?" Tyler asked.

"Where's Molly?" Ali gasped. *The spell worked,* she thought. *I did it!*

"She's still small," Tyler said. "I don't know where she is." Mrs. Hopper squirmed in his grip. She reached out a hand toward Ali, but Ali stepped back, out of reach. The fairies were disappearing into cracks and crannies. The only ones left in view were the few Michael was holding.

"Let us go, you monster."

"You got what you wanted."

"Oh, the stink!"

"Should I let them go?" he asked. "Ow!" He opened his hands and the fairies jumped down. Before Ali could say anything, they had all disappeared. "Where's Jennifer?" Michael rubbed his sweaty hands on his pants.

"She's gone!" Ali cried. "They made her small." She

put a hand on her head and looked around. "They weren't supposed to make her small."

"They weren't supposed to make *any* of us small," said Tyler, squeezing Mrs. Hopper tighter.

A fairy appeared on Mrs. Hopper's shoulder. She was still carrying the hairpin as if it were a royal scepter. "The spell needed a full-sized human," said Bunny. "A slave for a slave, that's how it works."

"The directions never said that!" Ali cried. "Plus, I sprayed Mrs. Hopper, not Jennifer."

"Mrs. Hopper is a fairy," said Bunny.

Imp, thought Ali. She glared at the Grand Miss.

"Furthermore, you and your friends have all broken the rules," said Bunny.

"No, I haven't! What rules? I read your directions and followed them." Fairies were streaming out of their crannies, flowing back into the salon. Some began climbing up Tyler's pants. This was not good.

"You haven't read them all yet," said Bunny.

"You can't hold me to something I haven't read! That's not fair!"

"You agreed."

"I didn't agree to this!"

"You agreed to follow the rules."

"Ah, get off me!" Tyler cried. He let go of the fake

Mrs. Hopper, who lunged at Ali and grabbed her around the waist and neck. She reeked of hairspray, and she grinned maniacally at Ali as Ali tried to squirm free. Tyler swatted the fairies, but they kept climbing up and up until they were on his head, and he disappeared.

Fairies crawled up Ali's legs, and then over her stomach, and then her chest, and this time she couldn't get away. "Michael, run!" she cried. But she wasn't going to give up. She shook her body as hard as she could and grabbed Mrs. Hopper's rubber arm.

Some fairies flew off her, but most held on. Mrs. Hopper's arm was surprisingly strong. Ali struggled, and then the pressure on her neck was gone. She shook herself. Where were the fairies? *Why are you thinking about this? Run!* She raced toward the door, but nothing looked the way it had. The door was nowhere and . . . what was that long, delicious-looking string?

ELEVEN

ALI stopped dead in her tracks. That giant
string was . . . *No* . . . it couldn't be. It was a hair,
and if the hair was large, then she must be small.
She looked down at herself. She was still wearing
her clothes. If she had shrunk, then so had they. She
felt the top of her head and breathed a giant sigh of
relief. Her bun was still there. At least being shrunk
didn't mean she had to be bald like them. But everything looked weird, magnified. *My eyes,* she thought.
They were as big as a fairy's! She turned, looking
for the other fairies, and there they were. They were
heading for her, a whole group of them. Was that
Mrs. Hopper's foot? It was giant! It was a mountain
of bare, scaly, fungus-infested, way-too-realistic fake-
old-lady toes.

"Michael! Michael! Michael!" she yelled at the top
of her tiny lungs.

"Ali!"

Ali turned toward the voice. It had come from the group of fairies that was now surrounding her.

"Ali!"

There she was—Jennifer—in the grip of two other fairies. She stood out because of her bun. Even with her eyes bulging out of her head and her giant tears dripping on the linoleum, she still managed to look gorgeous. Behind her, in the grip of more fairies, were Molly and Tyler.

"Thanks for trying," Tyler called. "It felt good to be big again!"

Someone scooped Ali up. The hand drenched her in sweat, and it *stank*. "Michael! Michael!" She was stuck to the pale, rough-yet-spongy skin.

"Get away! Get away!" Was that really Michael's voice? It sounded strange, so large and deep. Ali squeezed herself up through the sweaty fist, using the stickiness to keep her grip. She poked her head through the hole at the very top. Her vision was clouded with the sweat that had dripped onto her bulging eyes, but the view was unmistakable: It was Crista! She was holding the giant door open with one hand and spraying the fairies with the other. On the can Crista was holding were the words EXTRA-STRENGTH IN-SECT REPELLENT.

The fairies raced around on the ground in front of Crista, frantic to escape the bug spray.

"Get the others!" Ali shouted, but Michael raced past Crista and out the door. His hand shook and his feet pounded, and every organ in Ali's body banged against her tiny bones. Her skull rattled, and she was almost ready to throw up whatever was left of her breakfast cereal when the motion finally stopped. Ali was flung one last time into the wedge between thumb and pointer finger, and she rose up with the hand to sit in front of a giant mouth. Instinctively, she shrank back. Michael's teeth were now crooked yellow mountains, and his breath was a smoky, rancid wind.

"Ali? Are you all right?"

She closed her eyes and put her hand over her nose and mouth.

"Ali, come on. Talk to me! Are you okay?"

She would have to remove her hand sometime. "I'm fine," she choked.

"Oh man, this got totally messed up." A bead of sweat dripped from Michael's upper lip, narrowly missing his fist.

Another giant face came into Ali's view. The face panted. "Oh, Ali, is that you?"

"Crista!" Ali held on to Michael's thumb with one arm and waved the other. "You saved us!"

"I wish I'd made it back sooner," said Crista.

"Bug spray," said Ali. "It was genius!"

"I don't think it really hurt them," said Crista.

"I hope it did!" Ali fumed. "I hope it killed every last one of them!" She paused. "I mean, except for Tyler and Molly and Jennifer." She leaned against the sweaty thumb. "I just made everything worse."

No one said anything.

"It worked for a minute, though. If we could only have gotten Tyler out of the Kingdome . . ." Ali put her head down. Her eyes were now so large that they rested on Michael's fist, leaving her forehead hanging in the air. Who cared if Michael stank? She deserved it. She'd put her best friend in danger and gotten Jennifer changed into a fairy. Jennifer had turned out to not even be so bad, coming along when none of the other people with wishes had wanted to help. Now how were either of them supposed to help anyone? They couldn't make anyone big again without making someone else small. The directions had neglected to mention that little issue.

She had wanted to find a way to save Molly and Tyler without breaking any rules, but *of course* it hadn't worked. How could she have been so stupid? If only she could have gotten her wish, she would have had the brains not to go running into the salon half-cocked.

"I'm so stupid," Ali moaned. "So so so stupid."

"You're not stupid," said Crista. "You're brave. You got everyone together to save people you weren't even really friends with."

"Stupid," Ali said, banging her giant eyes against Michael's fist. "Stupid stupid stupid."

"It's going to be all right. We'll think of a way out of this," Crista said.

Silence.

"Right, Michael?"

Michael sighed, unfortunately with his mouth open. "Sure we will."

"You're worried about your wish, aren't you?" Crista asked, her voice rising. Oh no. Her rants were bad enough when Ali's ears were normal sized. She covered them, but she could still hear. "After what just happened, all you can think about is, 'How is she going to grow all those fairies for me now? How can I become some big sports star?' Never mind that Ali's a fairy now, thanks to you."

"Thanks to me?" Michael's fist widened, loosening his grip on Ali.

Ali grabbed on with both arms.

"Thanks to *me?*" Michael ranted. "I helped, didn't I? I risked everything to save those idiots who couldn't follow some stupid rules!" He waved his hand in the air.

"Stop!" Ali screamed, slipping farther and farther into his fist.

Michael slapped her from one hand into the other, plunging her into the overwhelming stench of stale cigarettes. Her head was completely covered, and Michael squeezed her as he continued defending himself. "Those other kids didn't come even though they got their wishes. I came! Now they think *I* broke the rules! They're going to be coming for *me* now."

"Help!" Ali pounded on the inside of Michael's fist. She was choking on the odor and not getting enough air.

"Michael, open your hand. She's suffocating!"

Michael opened his hand flat. Both giants peered down at Ali.

Ali gasped for breath. She wanted to collapse into the hand, but the fear of the smell and getting even more sweat on her kept her standing.

"Did I hurt you?" asked Michael.

"No," said Ali. "Thanks for rescuing me." She was now covered in sweat and leftover cigarette juice, and her organs had all been rearranged by the run, but at least she was alive and she wasn't a fairy slave. *It could have been worse*, she told herself. Not much worse, but still. She wasn't ready to give up. *Giving up is not Alison E. B. Butler's style,* she thought.

"What are we going to do now?" asked Michael.

"I still have to feed my fairies," said Ali.

"Are you serious?" Crista asked. A storm of spit landed half an inch from Ali. Crista's giant, contorted features hung in front of her. "What else can they do to you? We should let those little monsters starve!"

"What about our wishes?" said Ali. "I'm not going to go through all this and then lose my wish. After what happened today, can't you see I need it?"

"Yeah," said Michael.

"Hey!"

"I mean . . . I didn't mean . . ." Michael's giant lips turned down, and his giant eyes widened into an oversized expression of terror.

Crista groaned.

"And what if there *is* something else they can do to us?" Ali said. "I don't know. I promised them I'd come back with the rest of their breakfast."

"Well, how are you going to do it like that?"

"I guess I need your help," said Ali. "Michael can't help me because it's against the rules."

"Of course," said Crista, raising both arms. "He can get you into all this trouble, but he can't help!"

"I wish I could," said Michael.

Crista set her hand next to Michael's. "Come on, Ali, we'll let Michael go back to hanging around outside the school."

Ali climbed onto Crista's hand. It was sweaty, but at least it didn't stink as much.

"I go to class," said Michael quietly, stuffing his hands into his pockets.

"Well, go then," said Crista. She carefully cupped her hands around Ali and began walking, leaving Michael standing on the sidewalk.

TWELVE

YOU have to come home with me," said Crista. She was sitting in the backyard with her back against the maple tree. They'd fed the fairies some more of Crista's hair, then argued about how to get hair for that night, and then begun arguing about where Ali was going to live.

"But what will my parents do? I have to let them know I'm okay." Ali was sitting on Crista's shoulder. Crista's hair, which was still below shoulder length, was just hanging there. It was covered in hairspray from having been in the bun before, but that just made it crispy and even more appetizing. Not that Ali had ever tasted hair. She just knew it was delicious. She swallowed hard, trying to block out the seductive scent.

"They'll step on you, is what. They can't see fairies, remember? They can't even hear anything about feeding them, apparently."

Crista shook her head just a little while she spoke. A strand of hair flew in front of Ali's nose.

"Then . . ." It smelled so wonderful. Chocolate and gummy bears and pizza and pork chops and angel food cake . . . "Then . . . we have to come up with a story, something so they won't worry."

"Like what?" asked Crista.

"I don't know. I . . . I . . ." Three hairs swung by Ali's face. She reached out for one, but missed. It was hanging right there, but her hand wouldn't touch it. She walked right up to it and held out her arms, and the strand wouldn't connect with her body. But she could *smell* the hairs, so much that she could *almost* taste them.

"Ali, are you listening to me?"

"What?"

"I said, your mom and Hannah are coming up the driveway."

Ali held her breath and turned to look. Despite her change in size, the distance she could see had actually increased. There were her mom and Hannah, walking from the driveway to the kitchen door.

"Mom!" Ali yelled. She knew they wouldn't be able to hear her, but she had to try.

"Mrs. Butler!" Crista called. She stood up, knocking Ali off balance, and headed toward Ali's mom.

Ali grabbed on to Crista's shirt with both hands as she fell, ending up dangling on Crista's chest. And there it was, right on the front of Crista's collar, only three body lengths up. A stray, gleaming, no-longer-attached-to-the-head hair. She could get to it if she jumped—she knew she could. She dug her feet into the fabric of the shirt. These fairies must be super-strong—she wasn't even breaking a sweat.

"Hello, Crista," said Mrs. Butler. "Did you leave something in Ali's room?"

"No, Mrs. Butler," said Crista, "It's about Ali. See, she, uh . . ."

Ali jumped. She overshot the hair and fell back, grabbing onto Crista's shirt just in time.

"Eee!" Crista twitched.

Ali swung beneath Crista's collar. The hair was so close. If she could just climb up half an inch . . .

"Are you all right?" asked Hannah, in a tone of voice that said she hoped not.

"I'm trying to help Ali," Crista snapped.

"Did she leave something behind at school?" Mrs. Butler asked.

Ali lifted her left foot as far as she could and set it down in a loose spot on Crista's shirt. She pushed herself up and grabbed farther up on the shirt, right over the piece of hair. She pulled herself up one more step. Holding on with her right hand, she used her left hand to stuff the hair into her mouth.

It was the most delicious thing she'd ever tasted.

"At school? No, she, um, I hoped she could stay at my house tonight. We have a project we need to finish," said Crista.

"Tonight? You mean she didn't say goodbye?" asked Mrs. Butler.

"Goodbye?"

"Ali was accepted to the Divvy School for Gifted Children," said Mrs. Butler.

Ali slurped the hair down. It went down easily, like a noodle.

"I can't believe she didn't tell you," her mother continued. "She won't be back before high school graduation."

"She's not at school," said Crista. "She's been turned into a Divvy-imp. The Divvy School is a trick. Can't you tell what's magic from what's real?" Crista's voice rose.

"My goodness, what a shock," said Ali's

mother. "I'm sorry you had to hear this way. Would you like to come in for a snack?" She unlocked the door and went inside, leaving the door open behind her.

"Hannah, can't you tell that something's wrong here?" Crista tried.

Ali searched for more stray hairs near her, but there weren't any. Suddenly she became fully aware of what Crista was saying. Pressed against Crista's shirt, she managed to turn her head just enough to see part of Hannah's face out of one eye.

"She went to some fancy boarding school for gifted children," said Hannah.

"She gets Bs and Cs," said Crista.

"She tested in or something," said Hannah.

"And she's not coming back until after *high school graduation*?" Crista said. "She's not coming back for any breaks?"

"That's the way the school works," said Hannah. "Sorry." She followed her mother inside the house, leaving Crista standing in the backyard.

Ali wanted more hair. There was bound to be hair inside the house. There was always hair in random places with three women around. She had to get inside. Without thinking, she jumped off Crista's shirt and landed on the grass. It didn't hurt at all to drop that far. She ran through the stalks, bounded up the steps, and had almost reached the kitchen door when it slammed shut. She screeched to a stop and looked up at the humongous flaps of peeling paint. Then the enormity of what she'd just heard hit her.

"Mom?"

On Ali's desk, a crumpled-up piece of paper slowly unrolled itself and smoothed itself out on top of a stack of schoolbooks.

Ali's mother fiddled with the window, making sure it was closed and locked now that her daughter was gone and no one would be coming into this room much. She didn't see the paper, or the books, or the clothes still hanging in the closet and peeking out of Ali's drawers.

You must never attempt to tell anyone who has
   graduated from 8th grade that fairies exist.
You must never attempt to harm a fairy.
You must treat hair products with respect.

Ali's mother hummed to herself as she left the room, closing the door softly behind her.

THIRTEEN

I'M not late," Crista whispered, kneeling on the ground in front of the fifth mound, which she had just finished building. "It's only eleven o'clock."

"We were afraid you had abandoned us," said Ringlet.

"Your friends should have thought of that before they turned *my* friends into fairies," said Crista. "You're lucky we're here at all."

Ali stood on Crista's shoulder. She had convinced Crista to put her hair up in the bun again, thank goodness. When the hair was on top of her head and all held up by spray, it was just a bit less tempting. Crista had given her a little hair earlier, after Ali's behavior in front of her mother and Hannah, but Ali was already ravenous again. She did not want any other food. Without even trying, she knew she would not be able to eat anything else. She needed hair.

Crista wiped her hands on her jean skirt and reached into her backpack.

"Hair. Hair," the fairies whispered.

Crista pulled out a plastic bag with the giant words ANNIE'S HIGH QUALITY WIGS on the front of it. "You owe me a lot of money," said Crista. "But it was either this or go sit in the movie theater with scissors." She pulled a wig out, a beautiful head of thick, black locks. "The lady said it was real human hair from India."

From the dirt where their mounds stood, fairies seeped into the grass, more and more of them. Pilose had said there were now forty-two, but Ali was losing count.

Crista put a paper towel down on the grass, then held the wig in her left hand and began cutting pieces of hair off it with her right.

The fairies swarmed onto the paper towel. "Hair. Hair. Hair."

Ali was supposed to wait until Crista fed her. She was not supposed to go anywhere near the other fairies, because didn't they want to capture and enslave her? But the hair was falling and the fairies were eating it, and it smelled like hair, and before she could stop herself, she had jumped down to the paper towel and begun gobbling the hair up.

It was not good hair. It was old and stale and rubbery tasting. But she was so hungry that it didn't matter. The hair kept falling, and she kept eating and eating, until she reached out for another strand and grabbed on to nothing. She stood with the others, in the middle of the crowd, all looking up at Crista, who stood over them with the now short-haired wig in one hand and giant, menacing scissors in the other.

"Ali, where are you?" Crista's eyes flitted over the group.

Fairy eyes turned toward her, but no one made a move. They stared, some of them with their mouths open. The ones nearest her pressed back into the others, leaving a space around her.

They're babies, thought Ali. *They're more afraid of me than I am of them.*

Pilose climbed onto Ringlet's shoulders and raised her arms.

"Ali?"

"No, it's not Ali," said Pilose. "It's Pilose. I'm one of the flock starters. You might be able to pass this stuff off on my poor infant charges, but you can't fool me.

You gave us old, stale hair. Barely better than cat hair, you well know."

"*I* don't know anything," said Crista. "How can you complain about getting free meals twice a day? My parents pay for the food *I* eat. Do you know how much real human hair wigs cost?"

"The babies won't thrive!" Pilose cried.

"It's what you'll get," said Crista. "Come on, Ali, let's go."

Pilose jumped down off Ringlet's shoulders and pushed through the crowd toward Ali. The others moved aside for her, but they kept watching Ali. The paper towel was a sea of fairy eyes.

"So, you invaded the Kingdome," said Pilose.

"Ali!" Crista peered down at them.

"Wait a minute," said Ali. She knew it would be smart to run away, but here was Pilose coming toward her. This little fairy was now taller than she was, and she now had her own facial features, distinguishing marks that Ali had never noticed before.

Pilose's face was long for a fairy's. Her narrow cheeks met in a sharply pointed chin. Her nose was also sharply pointed, and it hung, beaklike, over her small, delicate mouth. The starlight reflected off her bulging bright blue eyes, and combined with the shine on her bald head, the effect was strangely beautiful. She wore loose canvas pants with a simple three-quarter sleeve T-shirt, causing her long wrists and fingers to stick out as she held a hand out toward Ali.

Ali hesitated for a second, then reached out and shook Pilose's hand. The fairy's grip was firm, neither too loose nor too tight.

Pilose smiled, showing a little row of perfectly white teeth.

"Hello," said Ali.

"Hello, Alison," said Pilose. "Welcome to our flock."

"I don't want to be part of any flock," said Ali. "I plan to become big again."

"You are still our child," said Pilose, "even though you've lost your size."

"Why do I like hair, then?" Ali asked.

"A child can take on attributes of fairies, just like fairies can take on attributes of humans," said Pilose. "Size matters quite a lot, you know."

"Not fairies, Divvy-imps," said Ali.

Pilose grimaced.

"Yes, I know," said Ali. "Your Grand Miss basically admitted it."

"Ali, stop talking to that fairy," said Crista. "We need to go home."

"Just a minute," said Ali.

"Would you like to come inside and see what you've built?" asked Pilose. "I can answer all your questions."

This was not a good idea. She shouldn't even be standing here with them. It was a miracle they hadn't carted her off to Mrs. Hopper's salon already. But now that she was down here among them and not in the middle of a fight, they didn't seem so scary. She only had to turn a little to see the five mounds that rose majestically above their heads. There was something warm and inviting about them. For the first time, she noticed little holes all up and down the sides of the mounds. Light was coming out of them, as if from windows.

"I'm going to go inside," she called out.

"You are not going in there!" said Crista. She reached down with her finger and thumb to pick Ali up, but Ali dodged.

"We will not hurt her," said Pilose.

"Really," said Crista.

"Yes, really," said Pilose. "And if we say we won't, we can't. It's one of the rules."

"Is that one of the rules you read, Ali?"

"No," Ali admitted. "Going inside just feels right. I know I'm going to be fine."

Crista let out a giant sigh. "Whatever you want, Ali. You have five seconds to change your mind." She folded her humongous arms and glared down. "Five, four, three, two—" She paused and glared. "Fine. See you tomorrow morning, Your Idiocy." She bowed her enormous head over her immense chest in the most sarcastic manner possible, then snatched her backpack off the ground and stomped away, shaking the fairies' little patch of ground.

Jared peeked over the fence, just enough to see Crista storming away. He ran his hand through his thin, wispy hair, letting the dandruff flakes fall around his shoulders. What exactly had Ali done to get shrunk by the evil fairies? Would she still be able to grow one hundred? Nothing could get in the way of his getting his looks back—and getting his revenge on his treacherous cousin Jonathan. He'd have to keep a close watch on Ali and her friend to make sure it all went as planned.

Jared grabbed his bike from where he'd leaned it against the fence. It was late enough that he could sneak into his house without running into his parents and seeing them try to hide the disgust in their eyes. He could handle a few more nights. But he couldn't wait forever. Jonathan was going to pay, just like anyone—kid or fairy—who tried to stop him. Smiling grimly to himself, Jared rode off into the night.

Bunny sat on the back of the salon chair, her dainty legs hanging over the edge, comfortably barefoot. She held her hairpin scepter in her left hand and surveyed her subjects. They stood silently at attention, waiting for her to speak. This was the way things were supposed to be.

"Subjects!" she cried regally. "I have good news to share. Lockner!"

The back door opened an inch, and Lockner marched through, holding his own hairpin and standing up straight and tall. Following him, fairies marched single file into the room. Sixty-one, sixty-two . . . Bunny counted them silently as they lined up. Ninety-eight, ninety-nine, one hundred.

Bunny smiled down benevolently. "One more flock for the Kingdome!" she announced.

The fairies cheered.

"We are so close to being big, I can taste the chocolate and roast beef we'll eat!"

The fairies cheered louder.

"Lockner, bring the child."

Lockner bowed to Bunny, then headed back for the door. He pushed it open, using both hands and straining mightily against its weight. A boy stood behind the door. He shifted nervously from foot to foot.

"You may enter, child."

The boy walked in slowly, all the time staring at the multitude of fairies standing before him. He glanced at Follica/Mrs. Hopper, who was kneeling in back of the group. Then he quickly glanced away.

"You have done well, child," said Bunny. "Now we will grant your wish. First choice: improvement or hex?"

"Um . . . improvement . . . please," said the boy.

"Which?" asked Bunny.

"Likability," said the boy. He shifted uncomfortably.

"Are you sure you wouldn't like mental acuity?" Bunny asked. "I hear you tried to use dried jellyfish instead of seashells."

The boy shook his head.

"Very well, then," said Bunny. "Likability it is. Come forward." She waved her scepter at the boy.

He stepped forward carefully, watching for errant fairies, until he was standing between Bunny and the rest of the Kingdome.

"Now hold still." She waved her scepter, and the fairies began climbing up the boy's jeans, up and up until they covered the top of his head (newly shaved, per directions), flocked onto his shoulders, and hung from his clothes in clumps.

> "On all their heads
> In all their beds
> On all their floors
> Through all their doors
> Yum! It comes from children
> Yum!"

As the fairies sang, they danced on the boy's head, lightly at first, then more and more frantically, until they were pounding their little feet on his bare skin.

He stood still, petrified.

> "Hair!"
> "Hair!"
> "Hair!"
> "Hair!"

As one, the fairies jumped off the boy onto the ground and scurried back toward Mrs. Hopper. Only Bunny and her trusty chancellor, Lockner, remained at the front. Lockner took the Grand Miss's free hand, and together they shouted, "HAIR!"

The boy's scalp began to glow, softly at first. It glowed brighter and brighter, until after a minute his scalp was lighting up the whole room. Of course, any adult walking by the shop just then would have seen nothing but a dark and deserted storefront, its red-and-white-swirled barber pole still and quiet next to the streetlight.

At the height of the brightness, hair suddenly shot through the boy's scalp.

The boy screamed and clutched his head.

The hair grew and grew until it came down to his chin, uneven and wild.

He clutched it, panting. "My hair."

"A beautiful crop," said Bunny to Lockner.

"Beautiful, Miss," said Lockner.

"Is that it?" asked the boy.

"Oh, yes," said Bunny. "You are very likable now. Everywhere you go, other children will crowd around you. You'll be invited to every party, and people will cry when you don't come."

The boy stood still for a second, staring at Bunny and Lockner with his eyes wide and his mouth dropped open. Then he ran for the back door and through it, never stopping to look back or say thank you.

"I'm not sure *I* like him," said Lockner.

Bunny chuckled. "We don't have enough magic for that."

FOURTEEN

I HOPE it's really one of the rules that you can't hurt me," said Ali. She knew she *was* being an idiot, but she couldn't help it. It felt right.

"It is," said Pilose. She smiled, and if Ali hadn't been so on guard, she might have thought the smile was genuine. Pilose spoke to the rest of the fairies. "You have nothing to be afraid of," she said. "Alison is our child. It is her responsibility to grow this flock and make it strong. She will not hurt us, because if she does, then she will only hurt herself." Pilose's smile grew wider, and Ali knew that though it might have been genuine, it was a warning.

"What exactly is a flock starter?" Ali asked.

"We are just old imps who channel the incarnation magic well. This is the magic that allows us to create new imps out of seashells and grass. We come from the beach originally, you know. We've multiplied using ocean things since before Impoliptus, the Great Imp who brought the magic that tied imps to children. My brother Ringlet and I—" Pilose reached out a long-fingered hand and waved Ringlet forward. He had a rounder face than Pilose and a short, stubby nose. He did not smile as he stepped just behind his sister. "—Ringlet and I make a good team. We started this flock." She frowned. "And many more. Ever since we un-enslaved ourselves from the chains of Divvy-imp magic, we've been starting flock after flock."

"You said you'd answer my questions," said Ali. "I want to know about Divvy-imps."

"We should go inside," said Ringlet.

The babies—who were almost as large as Pilose and Ringlet and were different only in the way they hung back from Ali—had huddled together in a bunch.

"Come," said Pilose. "You must see the home you've built for us."

Ali entered the mound simply by standing on top of it. One second she had a view of the forest of the backyard grass, and the next she was somewhere else entirely. And had she not *known* she was inside a mound made of dirt and seashells, she would never in a million years have guessed it.

The inside was mound-shaped, but the ceiling appeared higher than the mound looked from the outside. An array of chandeliers hung from the ceiling, so far up that they looked tiny. Some hung higher and some lower, so that they dangled haphazardly, more like wind chimes than proper light fixtures. But light was coming from them, and somehow it was enough light to fill the entire interior of the mound.

The floor, too, appeared much larger inside than out. There was no sign of the dirt the mound was made of. The floor was shiny linoleum like the inside of a high-class department store. Along the wall to Ali's left was a row of five bunk beds, not the standard bunk beds with one little mattress stacked on top of another and a flimsy ladder, but grand affairs. The full height of a fairy separated the bottom bunks from the tops, and over the top bunks there were fancy canopies, which must have been held up by magic, as there were no poles underneath them. At the head of the room was a full-sized four-poster with its own grand canopy.

On the right side of the room was a long table—long enough to seat not only the ten babies that lived in this mound, but all forty-two. The table was laid with a feast. Ali saw slabs of meat, stacks of bread, piles of fruit, and mounds of chocolate at regular intervals—and no vegetables anywhere.

Ali would have asked what the point of all the food

was if they only wanted to eat hair, but first she had to ask about something more pressing. After standing on top of the mound, she had appeared here on the floor right in the middle of a pool table. Not *on* the pool table, but *in* it. She waved her arms around and found that they went right through the pool table, though the table looked every bit as solid as a normal one.

"How am I doing this?" she asked, flapping her arms.

"The table is not really there," said Pilose, who nevertheless was standing just outside it. "Neither is the rest of it." Pilose waved a long arm at what filled the room between the bunk beds and the dinner table—a motley assortment of things to play with. There was a Ping-Pong table, a badminton set, a volleyball court, and, in the distance past the four-poster bed, a baseball field. In between these games were slides of varying heights, jungle gyms, free-standing bars, and swing sets. When Ali tried to look closely at them, she realized that there were far too many games for the space, but she couldn't quite focus on them. They were all there somehow, going on and on into the distance.

Ali stepped out through the side of the pool table to stand next to Pilose. Ringlet was off near the bunk beds, getting the baby fairies settled.

"The babies can't control their magic yet," said Pilose. "They create things they want, but they don't have the power to make them real." Pilose stared at the phantom games as she spoke.

"Can *you* make things real?" Ali asked.

"Small things, for a short time," said Pilose. She pointed to the bunk beds.

"I don't believe you," Ali said. "I think you can do lots of things. You made Molly and Tyler and Jennifer and me small."

"We have more power when it comes to children," said Pilose. "But our powers over children aren't for us. They're for the sake of just deserts."

"Oh, come on," Ali said. "There's nothing *just* about making us small. You want to do it because you're evil!"

"Evil is relative to circumstance," said Pilose, raising her nose high in the air.

"What is that supposed to mean?" asked Ali.

"I never set out to be more than naturally evil," said Pilose. "I was a Divvy-imp. Like all Divvy-imps, I doled out punishments to children who deserved them and rewards to children who did the right things. I followed the rules, and I never wanted any more."

"So what happened?"

"Bunny happened," said Pilose. "She styled herself Grand Miss Coiffure—because the un-enslavement spell required hair, you see. She knew that hair held great power. She wanted to be more than a Divvy-imp. 'Why should we be enslaved to the behavior of children?' Bunny asked. 'Why should we be forced to give rewards?' Many Divvy-imps agreed."

"But not you?" Ali asked.

"Never mind that," said Pilose. "Anyhow, Bunny botched the spell. She thought, 'the more hair the better,' so she used a whole ponytail instead of a single hair. We're un-enslaved, but all we can eat now is hair. We're hardly enjoying ourselves."

"You didn't eat hair before?" asked Ali. She still had only the vaguest idea of what a Divvy-imp was. What exactly had they done to punish and reward children?

Pilose smiled dreamily. "We feasted at the human tables," she whispered. "Roast beef, pork chops, oranges, ice cream. Anything they had, we had—and when you are small, there is always enough."

"But what did you do to children?" Ali asked. "You keep saying you'll tell me, but—"

Just then, a great moaning came from the bunk beds. All ten of the babies were crying at once.

Ringlet hurried over to Pilose and Ali, slipping

through a tetherball pole on his way over. His eyes were glassy, and he was holding his stomach. "That hair is making them all sick," he said, glaring at Ali. "A stale old wig! Are we animals?"

"How could it matter?" said Ali, remembering how it *had* tasted stale. "All hair is dead anyway. It's no different in a wig than off somebody's head. And I'm not . . . oooh . . ." Ali's stomach churned. Maybe the wig hair *was* bad. Maybe she was going to throw up.

"I'm going to check on the other mounds," said Ringlet. "Ugh." He walked slowly back toward the bunk beds, passed them, and walked straight through the wall.

"How did he . . . oooh."

Pilose put her arm around Ali. She was looking a little green herself, but she pushed Ali toward the four-poster bed. They passed through the nonexistent games, and Ali found that the distance over which they traveled was not nearly as great as it had appeared. By the time they reached the bed, Ali's head was pounding and her stomach was churning even more.

"Lie down, Alison, and I'll tell you a story," said Pilose. She threw open the covers, and Ali needed no more encouragement. She slipped into the bed, curled into a ball, and closed her eyes.

FIFTEEN

We were happy to be imps, once," said Pilose. Her voice was far away and breathy, as if she were struggling for her words, maybe struggling with indigestion, too.

Ali's head spun. She kept her eyes closed.

"Ringlet and I—our names were different then, proper imp names—we lived in this very house. We were here long before you and your family moved in."

As Ali held on to her stomach, she felt even dizzier. She almost didn't hear Pilose's words anymore. Instead, she felt like she was *inside* the scene.

Two imps sat on a step in the middle of a staircase. It was carpeted with brown shag, unlike the white fluff in the house Ali knew, but the shape was the same. The imps were clearly Pilose and Ringlet, but Pilose's cheeks were chubbier, more like her brother's. Ringlet wore simple cloth overalls, while Pilose wore a loose, plain light blue dress. Both imps had hair. Pilose's was long and dark and flowed down her back in curls, and Ringlet's was short and spiky, not greasy with hair products but naturally wild.

A little boy bounded down the stairs. Oblivious to the imps, his bare foot landed right on top of them but passed through them harmlessly. Suddenly, his body froze, hanging in mid-run above the staircase. His bed hair and striped pajamas combined with the smile on his face to give the impression of action, even more so because it was frozen.

"What a day Andy had," said Ringlet. "He put salt in the sugar bowl, surprising both of his brothers. He tripped Jay on these very stairs."

"Resulting in no injury," said Pilose.

"Yes, but there could have been." Ringlet sighed. "Still, he stood up for a littler boy in school. He gets points for that."

Pilose sighed, too. "Only a stage-one punishment, I'd say."

The boy began moving again, and as he reached the bottom of the stairs, he tripped and fell face-first into the carpet. Just in time to witness this, two older boys bounded down the stairs behind him. They laughed, and Pilose and Ringlet grinned.

The scene shifted. Pilose and Ringlet were now at the dinner table with a mother, a father, and the three boys. They were eating beef stew with potatoes and carrots and onions. *Steam rose from a large pot, and the family chattered as they spooned the mixture onto their plates. The imps shoveled food into their mouths from the mother's plate, gravy dripping down their bodies.* Ali could smell the meat as if she were in the room with it. Along with the stew there were biscuits and jam. The aroma of strawberry pressed into Ali's nose, mixing with the fresh biscuit and stew smell until she was positively starving. The discomfort she felt after eating the bad hair was far away, back in the dismal present with Pilose's voice.

Now the imps were in a bedroom. The position of the closet and the size of the window showed Ali that it was hers. Instead of her single bed, there was a bunk bed on which the two younger boys slept. The youngest one was on top, an arm and a leg hanging precariously over the edge. The imps had their own set of bunk beds, out in the middle of the floor where a moonbeam coming in through a gap in the blinds bathed them like a spotlight. Pilose was on the top bunk. She lay on her back with her arms folded over her stomach. She breathed in and out deeply in sleep, and she was smiling. Her black hair framed her beautiful, silent face, as if she were Snow White.

Ali opened her eyes. She hadn't realized that she

had fallen asleep, but now the crick in her neck and the sour but less violent ache in her stomach showed her that time had passed. She sat up slowly in bed—and gaped at the scene before her. Pilose sat silently next to her, frowning.

The illusory games were gone. The table with the food was gone. The floor in front of them was nothing but bare dirt. A worm slithered up through a hole only a short distance from Ali and, paying no attention to them, oozed across the room and away. It was as large as a sea monster, a slimy, disgusting animal right in their sleeping space. The canopy above the bed was gone, too. The bed Ali lay on was nothing but a pile of cloth, and the scrap that covered her might have come from the pile of torn T-shirts her mother kept in the closet for rags.

The ten baby fairies were no longer on bunk beds, but huddled together on piles of cloth. Ostensibly, there was a pile for each fairy, but they had ignored the distinctions and were all wrapped in a ball as one. A barefooted fairy leg stuck out from the bundle, shivering in the morning cold.

Ali pulled the scrap of cloth over herself for warmth. "What happened?" she whispered.

"This is how it is," said Pilose. "Our magic and

our hopes keep the mound looking splendid when we are awake, but when we sleep, things go back to how they are."

"Is this why you wanted me to stay?" asked Ali.

Pilose nodded her bald head. "You call us evil. We only want what *you* have. We know what you have because we used to live there with you."

"What do we have that's so great?"

"Don't you know?" Pilose exclaimed. "You have toys and games and birthday parties and junk food, and you can go anywhere you want without being forced to help anyone else."

"I can't go wherever I want," said Ali. "I have to go to school, and my parents make me go to bed early. They're always telling me to be nice to other people."

"Yes, but you don't *have* to be nice," said Pilose. "We *had* to reward children when they were good. If we didn't, we'd itch terribly, worse and worse until we gave in. There's a difference between being told to do something and having to do it."

"You laughed when you punished children," said Ali. "Is that what you really want? To be able to punish us without ever giving rewards?" She wasn't sure she was supposed to have seen what Pilose had described so vividly. Surely Pilose hadn't told her they had laughed at the boy falling, but Ali remembered the fairies' grins as if she'd seen them herself.

"We'd rather not have to worry about children at all," said Pilose. "I don't want to hurt you." Pilose stared at Ali with those big eyes, and her mouth turned down in the saddest of melodramatic frowns.

"But you want to keep the magic," said Ali. "Just in *case* you want to hurt us?"

"We've earned it," said Pilose. "Why should fairies and trolls and unicorns and all those kinds of people have magic and not us?"

"Is that why you said you were fairies?" Ali asked. "Because they have more magic than you?"

"Have you ever heard of a Divvy-imp before?" asked Pilose.

"No," said Ali.

"And what do you think of when you hear *imp*?" Pilose asked.

"I don't know, like a mischievous creature, I guess?"

"What about when you hear *fairy*?" Pilose demanded, leaning in toward Ali.

"Like, Tinker Bell? Something with wings?"

"Something majestic!" Pilose cried. "Something dangerous. Something that might lure you away to another world and trap you there forever, or worse. No 'imp' ever scared anyone. Who wants to grow a hundred imps?"

"I didn't think fairies were scary until people said *you guys* were fairies," said Ali.

"Really?" Pilose smiled.

"Really," said Ali. "Besides, kids aren't growing you because you're fairies, they're growing you because they get wishes."

"I guess," said Pilose, folding her arms. "It's just embarrassing—being something nobody ever heard of. Nobody ever tells stories about Divvy-imps. 'Fairies' sounds more impressive. And yes, if you must know, they *do* have more magic."

Another worm slithered out of the wormhole. The first worm had reached the edge of the mound and was burrowing its way through, while the second one wriggled along, its pink skin writhing so that its veins showed.

"So you want me to feel sorry for you or something?" asked Ali, pulling the scrap of rag around her shoulders. "You've made me small like you. You've made my parents forget about me." In the dismal, dirty mound, it was hard to hold back the feelings Ali didn't want to feel. Her parents didn't miss her. She turned away from Pilose so the fairy wouldn't see her trying to hold back her tears.

"That's not my fault," said Pilose. "Grownups can't know about any magical creatures. That's a law of nature. What would happen if grownups could know about us?"

"I don't know," said Ali.

"Life would be no fun for anyone, that's what," said Pilose.

"Life is no fun right now," said Ali. "I guess you're going to send me to the hair salon to be a slave like my friends. That'll be great." Ali was dimly aware that she should be jumping out of bed and running, but she didn't want to. She just wanted to lie there in the filthy rags forever.

"The Grand Miss can find her children somewhere else," said Pilose. "If you stop feeding us, the babies will starve. They'll wink out of existence as if they'd never been." There was a great sadness in Pilose's voice, and this time Ali thought it was real. "The babies are only copies now. They eat and they shiver with the cold, and they speak and feel as we do, but when the flock is complete, they truly become whole imps. There is nothing in the world like seeing their eyes light up with the full magic of life. If you become a slave, that will never happen for these babies. They will die."

Ali rolled over to look at Pilose. The imp's eyes were filling with water. "I never thought about that before," she said. "I thought that making us grow a hundred was just a stupid rule."

"It's not stupid to me," said Pilose. She turned to watch her babies, who were stirring in their bunks now.

"What happens to *you* if I don't finish growing them?"

"I'll have to start another flock," said Pilose. "I'll always start another flock." The fairy's eyes squeezed shut.

"Do you not like being a flock starter?" asked Ali.

"It takes so much energy," said Pilose. "We get as ravenous as the babies—more. You saw how we behaved—banging against the jar, screaming. I hate degenerating that way."

As Pilose spoke, one of the baby fairies walked over to Pilose and Ali's bed of rags. He was wearing ragged pajamas now, full of holes and too short for his arms and legs. "Hair," said the baby. His bald head glistened with dew.

"Soon," said Pilose. Her voice was soft, and she smiled at the baby imp. The expression changed the fairy's whole face from somber to gentle.

Ali hoped Crista would come back. They fought all the time, and Crista would storm out, and then the next day everything would be fine. But what if this was different? What if Ali had finally pushed Crista too far? Then she'd really have no one. Just as Ali had convinced herself that Crista wasn't coming back, that she was all alone and about to starve besides, she smelled it. Before she'd gotten shrunk, she would never have had any idea that hair smelled like anything except shampoo. But now it smelled almost exactly like roast beef.

"Hair," Ali whispered.

Bunny and Lockner stood in the closet, watching the three slaves polishing the giant seashells with mousse. Bunny was perched on a cardboard box so she'd stand above her subjects. Lockner stood at the foot of the box, holding the Grand Miss's hairpin scepter.

"You—the new one—quit your whimpering and get back to work."

Standing in front of a shell that was only half crusted, Jennifer wiped tears from her eyes.

Bunny pointed with one finger, raising her arm so that her green wrapping-paper dress crinkled dramatically. "There's no crying in the Kingdome!"

Jennifer sniffed and picked up her rag again. Silently, she began to rub the rest of the mousse into the shell.

Lockner, still holding the scepter in one hand, climbed awkwardly up the back of the box, where the imps had cut out pieces of cardboard to form a makeshift ladder. "Miss," he whispered when he reached her, "we are closer than ever to our goal. We need only two more flocks to have enough power for the Replacement."

Bunny smiled and took her scepter from Lockner. "Soon we'll be able to put mousse in our wigs." She patted her bald head with her free hand.

"Yes, Miss," said Lockner. "But we have only three children." He inclined his head toward the three slaves.

"We'll have Alison Butler," said Bunny, "but first she needs to finish her flock. I won't go losing another crop so far along." She stared down her nose at Lockner, despite their being the same height. "If you think she'll run off, you forget the greedy nature of children. She thinks she'll get her wish *and* be big again."

"We still need a fifth," said Lockner.

"Michael Landis has already broken the rules," said Bunny. "By the time the Kingdome is complete, we'll have enough children for the spell."

Lockner smiled. He shifted inside his Happy Birthday wrapping-paper pantsuit. "Do you think we'll need wigs, Miss? Isn't it possible we'll grow our own hair back once we're big?"

"Everything is possible, Lockner." Bunny and Lockner exchanged thin, bald-headed grins.

SIXTEEN

Pilose grabbed Ali's arm, and before Ali understood what was happening, they were on top of the mound along with all ten of the babies. On the other four mounds, babies were spilling toward Crista's large form. There seemed to be more than last night's forty-two.

Ringlet ran up the mound toward them. "Only six more imps this morning," said Ringlet, his face red. "That hair was useless except for making us sick."

As Ringlet fumed, Crista pulled another wig out of her backpack. Pilose groaned, but the babies rushed forward toward it.

Ringlet ran down the mound. "Stop, stop—don't eat that!"

The babies slowed their run and looked back at him, their eyes bulging with hunger.

"Don't you remember how sick you were? Babies . . ." he muttered. Then he looked up at Crista. "You made the whole flock sick with that old wig!" His voice sounded deep and real to Ali now, not high and squeaky. And his anger made perfect sense. The hair *had* been bad.

"You said you ate hair, so you got hair," Crista's giant voice boomed. "The great Alison E. B. Butler may be willing to cut her own mother's hair, but I'm not." Oh no. The full name. Crista was still mad.

"I'm sorry, Crista," said Ali. Her voice sounded tiny in her own ears. "We appreciate your help, but the hair did make us sick."

Crista shoved the wig back into her bag. "Fine! I'll just get my money back." She stood up.

"Wait! Crista, don't go!" Ali shouted.

"Oh, do you want to get away now? Didn't you have a nice night with your new friends?"

Ali glanced at Pilose. She was pretty sure that Pilose wasn't going to drag her to the Kingdome and make her a slave, but she also wasn't eager to spend the rest of the day with the worms. Plus, it would be hard to come up with a new plan to save Tyler and Molly and Jennifer—and herself—with the fairies right there.

A large clump of hair dropped in front of the

mounds. The sky above Ali darkened as giant legs stepped over her and landed next to Crista.

The babies ran for the hair. Ali couldn't help it. She ran after them. She heard the voices in the background, but nothing was going to stop her from devouring her fair share.

Pilose spoke with her mouth full. "You aren't supposed to help."

"I know that, no thanks to your too-late directions," said Michael. "But I already went along with Ali's scheme to rescue Tyler and Molly. Your friends are coming after me no matter what I do now. And I want my wish. If Ali grows her flock, you still have to give it to me, don't you?" He wasn't yelling, but his voice was so loud that Ali would have put her hands over her ears if she weren't stuffing her face with hair. She was dimly aware that the hair she was eating was wet, obviously drain hair, while some of the babies were picking apart clumps that looked like they'd come out from under a sofa along with enough dust to choke a vacuum. But coming from a disgusting place didn't make the hair any less delicious. This morning it was like gummy bears. Sweet and tender gummy bears that exercised your teeth but never stuck. *Mmmm.*

Pilose stuffed a clump of hair into her mouth and considered. "It's never happened," she said. "When the children break the rules, the Grand Miss is able to take them. No one has ever broken the rules and then grown a flock."

"So we can do it," said Michael.

"I'm surprised you're still big," said Pilose. "They probably couldn't stand your smoke stench. But it won't last—Bunny will take you."

"Let her try it," said Michael. "Hey, Ali!"

Ali slurped up her last strand of hair. The fairies had done away with the rest and were now staring up at Michael and Crista, their eyes begging for more.

"Are you all right down there?" Michael asked.

"I'm fine," said Ali. *Except for being a fairy.*

Michael reached down and grabbed Ali between two fingers. Fortunately, he used the hand he hadn't been holding his cigarette with. It was almost clean. She wanted to be mad, but she was glad he'd made the decision for her. There was some strange force trying to tie her to those fairy mounds.

Michael dropped her into the front pocket of his shirt. The pocket was too deep for her to reach the top, but she jumped and was just able to catch the flap of fabric. She pulled her head over the edge and caught a view of Crista's receding back. Her above-the-shoulders hair fluttered unevenly as she stalked off.

"Crista!" Ali yelled. But Crista didn't stop. Maybe she hadn't heard Ali yelling, but Ali bet she had. "Thank you for bringing the hair!"

Crista still didn't stop.

"Forget her," said Michael. "She never made any agreement with the fairies, so she's probably safe. We need to worry about us."

"Pilose didn't try to enslave me," said Ali. She told Michael what she'd seen in the fairy mound. How the fairies were miserable waiting for the flock to grow.

"That's just because you haven't finished growing the flock yet," said Michael. "That little imp won't care about you then."

Ali had to admit that he was right. "So what are we going to do about it? The directions said—"

"Don't tell me!"

"What does it matter now? You've tried to hurt them, and you've given hair to my flock. You're screwed unless we use everything we've got."

"Yeah, I guess I am." Michael thudded down the sidewalk, ignoring a man who stared at him and stepped into the street to get out of his way.

"Anyway, it's not what the directions said, it's what they didn't say. Like the fact that the 'full-sized human' becomes a fairy slave to replace the kid you rescue. We need to ask the directions again—how to make a kid big again *without* making someone small. I think it's all in how you ask the question."

"We have to stop them from making me small, too," said Michael. "And how do we know that if we make you big, they can't just make you small again because of all the rules you've broken?"

Michael left the sidewalk and headed in toward the school. Crista was standing in front of the main doors, waiting for them.

"What's wrong?" Ali asked.

This time, Crista didn't pretend she hadn't heard. "Look."

"Look at what?" Michael passed Crista and pushed through the front doors. It was unnaturally quiet inside. Kids were just standing around, glancing nervously at one another. No lockers slammed, no voices shouted. No one ran down the hall. It seemed like everyone was scared silent. And *all* the boys had their heads shaved. *All* the girls were wearing the fairy-approved bun.

SEVENTEEN

ALL the kids stared at Michael.

"He's got one in his pocket!" someone cried.

Girls started screaming and running away down the main hall.

Four boys surrounded Michael. They were mean kids—the type of guys Ali had thought Michael was friends with. But they glared at him like he was an ant. One of the boys was Jonathan Yeager, the guy who had hexed his own cousin. He was about a foot shorter than Michael, but he got right in Michael's face.

"Why're you bringing them in here?" he said.

"Why is everyone suddenly afraid now?" asked Michael. "Plus, it's just Ali Butler." He pulled Ali out of his pocket and held her in front of Jonathan's face. His fingers pinched Ali's ribs so she could barely breathe.

"Put me back in your pocket, you moron!" Ali squeaked.

Michael dunked her back in.

"I'm not afraid," said Jonathan. "I just don't want everyone in the whole school trying to get them. This one screwed it all up." He poked the pocket Ali crouched in, narrowly missing her.

Ali jumped up and held on to the edge of the pocket again. "Stop that!"

"You better give her fairies to *me*," Jonathan continued. "Why'd you give yours to her anyway? I thought we were friends, man." Jonathan was the one eighth-grader in the school who was older than Michael, since he'd been held back twice. He was also one of the kids who tended to hang around across the street instead of actually coming to school. Ali wouldn't have been surprised if he was still around and able to grow his flock into next year.

"But that's not fair," Ali squeaked. "You already got a wish. It's not my fault you wasted it on a hex."

"Shut up, tiny," said Jonathan. "I'm getting an improvement too. I didn't see anything in the rules that says I can't grow two flocks."

"Who are *you* calling tiny? What are you going to wish for anyway, the IQ of an ostrich?" Ali squeaked.

"You stinky little—" Jonathan reached for Ali, but Michael stepped backward, and at the same time, the bell rang.

Vice Principal Johnson walked by. "To class, boys."

"You better have them for me after school," Jonathan said, leading his pack off. The crowd of kids who'd been watching the scene slowly dissipated, and Michael, to Ali's surprise, headed to class.

Ali crouched in Michael's pocket for the slow three hours until lunch. The voices of the kids were strangely subdued. Every time she peeked out, she saw kids glancing sideways at them, whispering, then turning away. But the scene in the cafeteria was a whole different story.

A group of kids stood right inside the doors, holding signs that read, STOP FEEDING EVIL FAIRIES!, DOWN WITH FAIRIES!, and SAVE OUR HAIR! They glared at Ali as she rode by.

"Doesn't anyone feel sorry for me?" Ali asked. "I only got shrunk because I was trying to help people."

"Oh, crap," said Michael. As he turned away from the kids with the signs, Ali saw what he was talking about. There was another group with signs, but these signs said things like, EQUAL FAIRIES FOR ALL!, STOP HOARDING WISHES!, and DONATE HAIR HERE—the last one above a large wicker basket lined with a garbage bag. As far as Ali could tell, no one had put any hair in the basket. What had happened to the hair that the boys had shaved off their heads? She could almost taste the gravy on the roast beef, and somehow she could also taste gummy bears. She leaned over the edge of Michael's pocket.

Crista came from behind them, brushing by without saying anything. She walked right up to the girl behind the basket, who was holding the DONATE HAIR HERE sign. "Have you lost your mind?" Crista yelled. "These fairies are evil! How could you possibly want them?"

"Shut up, Crista," said a girl holding a sign that said, BE FAIR, GIVE HAIR! "We know you have some. Otherwise, why do you have short hair all of a sudden?"

"I can't get my hair cut?" Crista shouted. "You guys are idiots. You should be listening to *them*." She pointed to the anti-fairy protesters.

"Give it up," said the girl. "We know you're best friends with Ali Butler. Obviously she helped you get some."

Crista turned around and glared at Ali. "Tell them how dangerous the fairies are." She waited. "Tell them!"

"I—Michael, can you move closer?" Ali waited for Michael to approach the pro-fairy kids. She cleared her throat. "They don't play fair," she said. "They promise you a wish, but if you break any of their rules, which they don't tell you, then . . ." She wasn't sure how much she could say without getting into more trouble, but she was already shrunk, and Michael was helping her. What more could they do? "Then they shrink you and make you slaves. I only just barely escaped, and I might never get big again. They've turned Tyler and Molly and Jennifer into slaves, and done something to Mrs. Hopper and replaced her with a giant fairy." She cleared her throat again. The girls holding the signs were staring at her like she was a spider they were about to stomp on.

"They made Jennifer beautiful," said one girl.

"And they made Barney Schmitt popular," said another.

"And now Natalie Buckmaster can sing," said a third.

"I could always sing," said Natalie, sliding between Michael and the girls. She sashayed through the cafeteria and into the food line.

"They're pretty much evil," said Michael.

"Tell us how you got them!"

"Give me some!"

"It's not fair!" the girls yelled. Other kids started crowding around them.

From behind, the anti-fairy kids weighed in. "Don't feed fairies! Don't feed fairies!" they chanted.

"Goodness gracious," said Vice Principal Johnson, pushing between the two groups. He ignored Michael and almost backed up into Ali's pocket.

She dropped inside.

"I've never seen kids with such strong opinions about library funding. Maybe we can buy both fantasy epics *and* an encyclopedia set. I'll take it up with the librarian this afternoon. Now please, let's have a nice quiet lunch!"

The kids grumbled a bit, but the situation outside the pocket gradually quieted.

"What are you doing?" Ali whispered.

"I'm getting some lunch," said Michael. "It sucks but I get it free."

"Can you find me some hair?" Ali asked.

"You really like hair as much as they do?"

"Yes! I don't understand it, but I'm starved *all the time*."

"Eee! Get your hands off me!" said a girl's voice.

"Sorry, he bumped into me," said Michael.

"I didn't!" a boy protested. From his trembling voice, Ali guessed he was a sixth-grader who'd heard about the terrible, scary Michael Landis.

Two smoke-stinking fingers appeared above the pocket, and four strands of long blond hair rained down.

"Back of the sweater," Michael whispered.

"FFanks," Ali said, mouth full.

Lockner pounded on the salon door with his tiny fist. As Mrs. Hopper opened the door, he raced to the back of the chair on which the Grand Miss perched. Huffing and puffing, he climbed the upholstery to her side.

"Well, what is it?" she asked, dipping her hand into

the pile of clippings next to her and stuffing a clump into her mouth.

"The children are revolting!" said Lockner.

"Dirty creatures, but we're stuck with them. What's your point, Lockner?"

"Not that kind of revolting, Miss—" Lockner gasped. "They're rebelling against the Kingdome. Some are agitating for the end of flocks!"

"The end of flocks!" Bunny exclaimed. "Those rugrats must not have heard about the wishes. You must do a better job of spreading the word."

Lockner began to sweat. "They know, Miss. They say the wishes aren't worth the risk of reduction in size. Not to mention . . ."

"What is it, Lockner?" Bunny snapped, stuffing another clump of hair into her mouth. "Spit it out."

"Well, Miss, they've also heard about the slavery part . . . and they know that the Kingdome is located here in the salon."

Bunny jumped to her feet and hopped in anger, her dress crinkling. "I told you to FIX THAT!"

"We can't erase memories, Grand Miss," said Lockner, stepping backward, pulling his head into his shoulders.

"WHO SAYS WE CAN'T!!" Bunny hopped and hopped, her face growing bright red.

"The magic!" Lockner cried. "It changes memories only when it suits the rules."

"I'M TIRED OF ALL THESE SILLY RULES!"

EIGHTEEN

ALI sat on her bed, now a vast expanse of purple flowers and smiley faces, a combination that had seemed hilarious only a few short days ago. Now the black smiley-face eyes were only blotches, their meaning erased by their immense size. She leaned against her pink unicorn, now bigger than a real horse. Its fake hair scratched her back, but she tried to ignore that and remember holding on to it when it had been a good friend and not a giant monster. It felt good to relax for a minute after the mad dash they'd made home from school in an effort to avoid Jonathan Yeager.

Pilose sat on top of the unicorn, her legs dangling over the side Ali was leaning against. Ringlet lay on his back near the unicorn's bottom, staring straight up at the ceiling, his arms crossed over his chest.

Michael sat on Ali's desk chair, while Crista paced up and down.

"Are you sure no one's going to hear us?" Crista asked.

"They all went to a movie," said Michael. "We have plenty of time."

"Going to movies like nobody's missing," said Ali. "I bet they wonder why they're suddenly so happy."

"It's just magic," said Crista. "In their real brains, they remember."

"Magic is perfectly real," said Pilose. "Why do humans make silly distinctions? It has rules and ingredients just like science."

"So their brains have really been erased?" Ali asked.

"Well, yes," said Pilose. "But magic can change their brains back, if the rules allow it."

"Whatever," said Crista. "Ali, your parents are going to remember you again."

"Yes, yes," said Pilose. "But first things first. We are all bound together now. You three have been feeding us together. That makes all of you our children."

"What do you mean by 'our children'?" asked Crista, stopping in mid-pace.

"Each flock must have one child," said Pilose. "That's the way it's always been. You three have mixed everything up. I can't be sure what the result will be."

"I'm not your child," said Crista. "I never signed one of your agreements. All I did was help my friend after you shrank her."

"I'm not a child," said Michael. "I'm fourteen." He slouched in his chair and tossed Ali's pink-haired troll pencil back and forth between his giant hands.

"You can see me, can't you?" Pilose scoffed.

Michael broke the pencil in two and slammed it down on the desk. "Just tell us whatever your big news is. We still need to get your hair for tonight."

"I'm trying to tell you," said Pilose. "Ali, where did you put your agreement?"

"It's in the desk drawer on the left," said Ali.

Michael opened the desk drawer and pulled it out. "She agrees to grow her fairies, pass on the flock starters, follow the rules. We know this already. So what?"

"Flip the paper over," said Pilose.

Michael did. He blinked.

"What?" Crista demanded, grabbing for the paper.

"I'm not sure you want to —"

"Just give it to me!" Crista ripped the paper

from Michael's hands. "WHAT?" Her face turned an abnormally bright shade of red.

"What does it say?" Ali asked, not sure she really wanted to know.

"It says:

'**And I also agree on behalf of anyone who might help me collect my hair that if any child feeds hair to my flock, that child shall also be bound by this Agreement.'

"Ali, did you know about this?"

"No, of course not!" Ali cried. "I only saw the front side. There wasn't any back side!"

"There's always a back side," said Pilose. "I guess you didn't ask to see it."

"I have to ask to see it?" Ali fumed. "I never agreed—"

"There are two stars on the front," said Crista.

"What?" asked Ali.

"After the line that says 'I will follow all the rules,' there are two stars. Did you ever stop to think about what those two stars meant?"

"I . . . um . . ."

"Didn't it ever occur to you to *read the fine print?*" Crista balled the agreement up in her fist and scrunched it until her knuckles turned white. She looked like she wanted to throw something, or hit something, or scream, or like her head was about to explode in a puff of smoke.

"Now you'll want to read your directions," said Pilose. "What have you done with them, Alison?"

"They're on top of the desk," said Ali. Her heart sank into her stomach. Something *else* that was not good was about to happen. So much for relaxing.

"You can't read someone else's directions," said Michael, but he picked up the sheet of paper anyway. "See, there's nothing . . . oh, crap." Michael brought the paper over to the bed and set it down next to Ali. Crista leaned in next to him. Ali thought she could feel steam rising off of her. Pilose and Ringlet peered over Ali's head.

Where the directions had been, there was now a picture. It showed a crudely drawn head with large eyes labeled ALISON BUTLER. But as soon as the group started looking at it, two other heads began to fade in. They were labeled CRISTA TRAYNOR and MICHAEL LANDIS. After only a few moments, the pictures of Michael and Crista were just as solid as the one of Ali.

Crista Traynor

Alison Butler

Michael Landis

Flock

Flock Starters

"I don't have curly hair," said Crista. "And why is my tongue sticking out?"

"Why do I look crazy?" asked Michael.

"My eyes!" Ali exclaimed. She put both hands to her head. "Why am I bald?"

"Is that all you care about?" asked Pilose. "It's not the faces that matter, it's the names. Your names are all here. And more important than that, you're all tied to my flock by the Hair of the Eternal Imp!"

"The Eternal Imp?" said Crista. "That's ridiculous."

"This is very serious," said Pilose. "You cannot cut

the Hair of the Eternal Imp except by seeing the flock grown — and maybe not even then."

"Who's the Eternal Imp?" asked Ali. "Impoliptus?"

"No," said Pilose. "Impoliptus is the Great Imp, the one who first tied imps to children, but he is only an imp. The Hair of the Eternal Imp is the magic that ties imps to children and children to imps, magic that Impoliptus only harnessed. Before we un-enslaved ourselves, it tied us to rewards and punishments. Now it ties children and their flocks."

"So *let's say* I'm tied to your flock somehow," said Crista. "So what? We'll finish growing your stupid fairies and be done with you."

162

"But you've broken the rules," said Pilose.

"I didn't break any rules," said Crista. "I've done nothing but help you."

"Turn the paper over," said Pilose.

Crista grabbed the paper, flipped it over, and dropped it back onto the bed. Carefully, Ali inched forward.

RULES BROKEN

1. Helping another child gather hair. (Crista Traynor, Michael Landis)

2. Feeding your flock your own hair. (Crista Traynor)
3. Attempting to harm a Divvy-imp. (Ali Butler, Crista Traynor, Michael Landis)

As they read, the word *Divvy-imp* disappeared and was replaced by the word *fairy*.

"Oh, shut up," said Ali. "We know already." After a second, *Divvy-imp* reappeared.

4. Attempting to tell an older person about ~~fair~~ Divvy-imps. (Ali Butler, Crista Traynor, Michael Landis)

"No way!" said Crista. "I fed *Ali's* flock my hair."

"We became your flock when you started feeding us," said Pilose.

"There wasn't anything about attempting to harm a Divvy-imp," said Ali. "I read all the directions, so I know."

"Did you read anything since you were shrunk?" asked Pilose.

"Well, no, but that wouldn't be . . . fair," Ali said. She closed her eyes.

"It was on the directions I read," said Michael. He glared down at Pilose. "And don't tell me I can't talk about what's on them, because we're all supposed to be tied to the flock now and we're all reading the same directions, right?"

"That's right," said Pilose.

"I know what to do," said Ali, opening her eyes again. She stepped onto the paper. "These directions have to answer my direct questions. And I know they're just going to try to trick me again, but I'm not going to let them. I'm going to get them to fix everything, starting with me." She looked down at the paper. "How can I make myself big again without causing any consequences? That means no making someone else small, and no hurting me or my friends *in any way*."

The directions page went blank. Everyone waited.

"Well?" said Ali, folding her tiny arms across her tiny chest.

Touch your fingernails together.
Touch your toenails together.
Think big.

"Think big?" Crista asked. "That's it?"

Ali sat down on top of the directions and pulled off her shoes and socks. "That's it," she said. "They had to tell me! I've got it all figured out!" She sat cross-legged, contorting herself in an attempt to get her left toenails to touch her right toenails. "It's not that easy to . . ." She huffed and puffed. As soon as this was over, she was going to start doing yoga. Finally, her toenails were touching. She pressed her right-hand and left-hand fingernails together. *Big,* she thought. *Big. Big big big big big!*

Suddenly her whole body began to itch. She squirmed and scratched her stomach. The itch was worst right in the middle of her body and radiated out into her arms and legs. Then her eyes began to itch, too. She squeezed them shut and rubbed them with one hand, still scratching her stomach with the other.

"Run!" Ringlet screamed.

Ali's right leg, suddenly giant, popped out from her body. Her left eye popped into her still tiny head. Then her head popped out, knocking into the unicorn. The unicorn fell away from her. She was a giant head and a giant leg on a teeny-tiny body. Her right eye popped in and stopped itching. She opened both her eyes. All she saw was her leg, dwarfing everything around it. "Are you guys okay?" she asked. What if she'd crushed them?

"We're fine," said Pilose. The imp's voice was tiny

again. That was wonderful. Now if only the rest of her could get big, too. *Pop.* That was her right arm. *Pop.* There went her left. *Pop.* There was her—

"Aaaa!" The weight of her newly grown midsection was too much for the edge of the bed she'd been sitting on. She fell with a thump onto the floor, face-down.

"Ali!" Michael and Crista each grabbed an arm and pulled her up.

Ali made it to her feet and pressed each foot gingerly against the floor. They seemed to be the right size. She looked down at her hands. They were the right size, too. Everything was in order. She breathed in deeply. She'd never been so happy to see her own body in her whole life. She was never going to take being a normal-sized human being for granted ever again.

Crista and Michael stared at her.

"What?" Ali asked.

Crista slowly patted the top of her head.

Ali reached up to feel her hair. Where was it? There was something right in the middle of her head, but—she raced to the full-length mirror on her closet door. There she was, exactly the way she used to be, except for one very important, very big thing. She was almost completely bald. In the middle of her head, at the very top, there was a teeny-tiny little bun, just exactly like the one she'd worn when she was fairy-size.

She marched over to the directions. "Why do I still have fairy hair?"

You asked to be big. Now you are.

"You . . ." Ali resisted the urge to ball the directions up. There was still something she needed to know. "Never mind that for now. You listed a whole bunch of things we all supposedly did. And now Pilose says we're all tied together and it's a big deal. So just tell us what the consequences are."

NINETEEN

CONSEQUENCES

For attempting to harm a Divvy-imp or attempting to tell an older person about fairies: slavery and increased proportional size of eyes or equal-level punishment (Divvy-imp choice).

For helping another child gather hair: entanglement in Hair of the Eternal Imp.

For feeding your flock your own hair: Just don't do it. The Great Imp is not responsible for the results.

"The Great Imp is not responsible?" asked Ali. "Who is this guy, a vacuum cleaner salesman?"

"He is the great Impoliptus, founder of the Divvy-imp line—" Pilose began.

"I know, I know," said Ali, "but this doesn't tell us anything. What's going to happen?"

"I've never seen these consequences myself," said Pilose. "Crista is the first child to feed a flock her own hair."

"Well, I never tried to harm any Divvy-imps," said Ali.

"You sprayed Follica with hairspray!" Ringlet said.

"Follica? You mean the fake Mrs. Hopper? It wasn't supposed to hurt," said Ali. Though she hadn't even thought to wonder if it would.

"And *he* shook a whole mound of us with his carcinogenic monster hands." Ringlet glared up at Michael.

"Get over it," said Michael. "All they had to do was turn Tyler and Molly back. They're lucky I didn't rip their little arms—urgh." Michael stopped mid-rant and clutched his head with both hands. "AAAAH!"

Ali stared at him. His hands seemed even larger than they used to be. Were they growing, or was his head shrinking? The hands might have been growing larger, but they were closer to Ali now. He was getting shorter. Definitely shrinking.

"Stop this!" Ali said. She grabbed Pilose and shook the imp. "Whatever you're doing, stop it!"

Michael's hands suddenly popped into a smaller

copy of themselves. He was now no taller than Crista, who had stepped back from him and was looking from side to side like she was searching for a weapon.

Ali shook Pilose.

"Stop shaking her! We aren't doing it," Ringlet said. "The magic is bigger than us. You've created an imbalance by having three of you and breaking so many rules. It's happening whether we want it to or not."

Ali dropped Pilose on the bed. Her tiny tuft of hair was burning. She felt stronger. A power flowed through her whole body. "I took on attributes of an imp," she whispered.

"What?" Crista asked. "What did you say?"

"I said, I took on attributes of an imp," Ali repeated, louder. "I still have my fairy hair, and that means I still have at least one attribute, and that attribute is *magic*." She reached out a hand to Michael. "Stop shrinking!" she cried.

Michael had shrunk a few more inches while she was figuring it out, but he didn't shrink any more. He took a deep breath and stared down at his hands, then at Ali. "You're taller than me!" As he turned his head back, his left eye began to grow.

"Stop!" Ali cried.

But the eye grew and grew until it was as large on

his face as hers had been only a minute before. As large as a fairy's.

He rubbed his eye. "Something itches."

Ali's fairy tuft of hair burned. Nothing else happened to Michael. He stood there, now shorter than Ali with one extremely large eye. Ali breathed a sigh of relief. At least she'd stopped him from getting tiny. But Michael didn't seem relieved.

"No, no way! This can't be real. It can't be!" Michael pushed Ali aside and put his nose up to the mirror. "My eye! I'm so short!" He turned back toward the bed.

Pilose and Ringlet were standing on the side of the overturned unicorn. From this distance, Ali couldn't see their expressions. The imps shrank back and held on to each other.

"What are you afraid of?" asked Ali, leaning over them. "What *else* is going to happen?"

"She fed us her own hair," said Pilose. "The consequences are unknown."

"Well, if it was such a big deal, why didn't you stop her?" asked Ali.

"It was too late," said Pilose. "*You* fed us her hair. We didn't know she was going to start feeding us herself. Plus, we were hungry." The fairy's voice had sounded so grown-up and rational when Ali had been small, too. Now Pilose was sounding just as childish and whiny as she always had.

"Right! *You* were hungry and the consequences fall on *us*."

"Ali."

Ali spun around.

Crista's eyes were growing.

Michael stepped back from her, as if it were catching.

"Crista!" Ali grabbed Crista's shoulders and focused on her tuft of hair. Her head felt like it was on fire. "Hang on. Just . . . *think big*. You're going to be—" Ali was holding on to thin air. "No! Crista?" She peered at the ground, but all she saw was carpet. "Crista!" She got down on her knees, careful to make sure that no fairy was in the way. She rubbed her hair, setting free her tiny bun. The tiny crop of hair stuck straight up like the plastic hair on her troll pencil. "Make her big again! Make her big again!"

"Oh my goodness," said Ringlet.

"I don't believe it," said Pilose.

Ali scrambled to her feet. "Is she over there?"

"No," said Pilose. "She's . . . back at the mounds."

"At the mounds?" asked Michael, inching his way over to Ali. "Why?"

Pilose and Ringlet exchanged a glance.

"You see," said Ringlet, "when a new fairy . . . er . . . imp is born into our flock, we sort of feel this . . . tingle."

"So?" asked Ali.

"Well . . ." said Ringlet.

"We think your friend has become an imp," said Pilose.

TWENTY

CRISTA! Crista!" Ali called. She and Michael were standing over the five mounds. Pilose and Ringlet rode on Ali's shoulders. Michael had his arms folded, and his giant eye looked like it was positively going to pop out with anger. Ali was none too happy herself. "Crista, are you down there?"

Fairies (*no, imps*, Ali reminded herself) came pouring out of the mounds. Imp after imp crowded forward onto the grass beneath Ali's feet.

"Hair!"

"Hair!"

"Hair!"

"Hair!"

"Hold on," said Ali. "Everyone calm down."

The imps pushed forward, crawling on top of her feet, hanging on to her pant legs. Fortunately, her clothes had grown back with her.

"No one is getting any hair until I talk to my friend

Crista. Now where is she?" Ali stomped her left foot, sending imps flying.

"Alison, stop that!" Pilose exclaimed. "You'll hurt the babies." She raised her voice and spoke down to the imps. "Listen to me. We'll be back with hair very soon. But we need to see this former child, Crista Traynor."

"Former child?" asked Ali. "You said I took on *attributes* of an imp when I was small. I was still a child, just like I am now."

"I believe this is different," said Pilose. "Ringlet and I felt an addition to our flock. We've been feeling them all day, granted. Surprising considering the quality of hair we consumed last night. But we felt a particularly strong ping when your friend Crista disappeared. Becoming a member of the flock is quite different from being reduced in size."

"Hair!"

"Hair!"

"We don't have any freaking hair," said Michael.

The imps shrank back and huddled together in a mass. Slowly, a single imp pressed through the throng of babies and out into the open, just beneath Ali's feet.

"Ali?" The imp was completely bald and had large, bulging eyes just like the others. But it was wearing a jean skirt and pink T-shirt just like the ones Crista had been wearing only minutes before.

"Crista! Are you all right? Oh, Michael, look, she's lost her hair. Crista, I'm so sorry. We're going to figure this out."

"It's all right," said Crista-the-imp. "There's nothing to figure out."

"What do you mean, there's—"

Michael tapped Ali on the shoulder.

She turned around. Ali's mother was coming toward them. "Ali, what are you doing out here?" she asked. "Michael Landis, I've warned you to stay out of our yard." She looked up as if Michael were still six feet tall, and she spoke to the air above his head. "We don't need you and your goon of a brother harassing our girls."

Hannah walked up behind Ali's mom, followed by Ali's dad. They'd all come from the car. Ali had been so absorbed in the latest crisis that she hadn't even heard them drive up.

Michael glared at Hannah. "Me and Deacon haven't been harassing you, have we?"

Hannah flipped her hair. "Not lately."

"Hair!"

"Hair!"

The babies seemed to have forgotten about being scared and were now crawling around Ali's feet.

"There are seventy-six now," said Ringlet. "We need to feed them soon or they'll start tearing each other apart."

"It can't be later than nine thirty," said Ali. "We're supposed to have until midnight."

"Their growth is out of control," said Pilose. "Ringlet is right. We need hair now."

"You are certainly not staying out until midnight," said Ali's mom.

"Aren't I supposed to be at boarding school?" Ali asked. "And don't you notice anything strange about the way I look?"

"I know it's been hard on you, having Crista leave," said Ali's mom, "but that's no excuse for losing sleep."

"So Crista's at boarding school now," Ali said, glancing at Michael.

"Never mind that," said Ringlet. "Just tell her anything. The magic will take care of the rest."

"I can't talk now," said Ali. "I have to get hair for the evil fairies."

"We'll plant the tomatoes over the weekend," said Ali's mom.

"Tomatoes?" said Hannah. "She said she was growing carrots."

Oh boy. "If they don't get their hair soon, I don't know what will happen." They were crawling up her pant legs. If only she didn't know they were babies. If only she hadn't just been their size.

"You can't trim a hedge in the dead of night," said Ali's dad.

"There's no hedge!" Ali yelled. "I need some hair! Hair!" She rubbed her tuft.

Something light landed on the bare part of Ali's head.

The fairies began jumping around wildly.

Ali looked down. Hair was falling onto the fairies' heads like rain. They opened their mouths to catch it and reached out their tiny hands. She looked up. It was falling from the sky, starting about fifteen feet above them. It fell around her and Michael and the fairy mounds in a cylinder shape, and it was all kinds of hair. Light, dark, curly, straight, coarse, fine, long pieces and short clips rained down.

"Holy Impoliptus!" said Pilose.

Hair. Ali held out her hands and caught a four-inch-long clump of fine blond hair. Before she could even think about what she was doing, she had stuffed it into her mouth.

Michael was doing the same. "Fried chicken and corn bread!" he exclaimed, grabbing more out of the air.

"Cinnamon bears," said Ali, grabbing a fistful of

clippings that were buoyed up by the wind. The hair she had swallowed stuck in her throat. She gagged and sputtered, but she couldn't stop herself from pushing in another mouthful. It tasted so good.

"Hair," said Pilose softly.

"All right then, we'll see you inside," said Ali's mother, and she walked back toward the house.

"Nice of you to trim the hedge, kiddo," said Ali's father, following his wife.

"Weff neffer had a hevv," said Ali, her mouth full of delicious, thick brown hair.

Ali suddenly realized that Hannah was still there. She reached into her mouth and pulled out a few stuck strands, wiped some stray clippings off of her face, and turned around to face her sister. The hair was still falling, but lighter now.

"Something weird is going on," said Hannah.

"It's none of your business," said Ali.

"Why don't you go find my goon of a brother," said Michael.

Hannah rolled her eyes.

"You sneak around with him all the time but you can't even defend him," Michael said, one eye bulging.

Hannah looked up above his head. "Mom's not going to change her mind. It's easier this way."

"You think you're better than us," said Michael.

Deacon's head popped up over the fence. "Shut up, dumbass. Hi, sweet pea." He smiled at Hannah.

She smiled back dreamily.

Deacon landed heavily a few inches from one of the fairy mounds. It looked like he was going to step right on it, but his foot stopped short in mid-air. "What the . . ." He pressed his foot against the air, but it stayed stubbornly aloft. He shrugged and walked around the mounds, putting his arm around Hannah. "Mikey's just mad because your sis gave him the brush-off. Over here all the time like a lovesick puppy, but she thinks he's just an overgrown pea-brain."

Michael seemed to shrink even farther.

Ali stared at him. It had never occurred to her that Michael might like her. Sure, she'd wondered why he'd been nice to her even though he was mean to everybody else. Michael had started being nice to Ali just like Deacon had started being nice to Hannah. Suddenly, she couldn't look at Michael. She looked down at the fairies. They had retreated to the dirt in front of their mounds and were lying in the now lightly falling hair. Their little bellies bulged out.

Pilose lay on Ali's shoulder. She groaned. "I think we ate too much hair."

"Better than too little," Ali snapped. How could Pilose complain after all this?

"The magic is wildly unstable," said Pilose. She grabbed on to Ali's neck and pulled herself to standing.

Ali wriggled against the itching. "So I don't have to worry about feeding you tomorrow morning?"

"We should have stopped them," Ringlet groaned. He was still lying on Ali's other shoulder.

Pop. Pop. Pop.

The fat babies jumped up and began running around, screeching.

"What's happening?" Ali got down on her knees. "Crista? Where are you?"

Pop. Pop. Pop. Pop. Pop. Pop.

"Eeeiiiyeeeaaaah!" the little imps screamed. Many of them ran for the mounds.

"Crista!"

"Babies are popping out of thin air!" Crista yelled. "I've got to calm the others down." She disappeared again into the melee.

"Babies out of thin air!" said Pilose. "Oh no, oh no."

"What's wrong with that?" asked Michael. "So we get to a hundred faster, and I can finally get my wish." He didn't look at Ali.

"I can't believe you're really gardening at this

hour," said Hannah. "Come on, Deacon, let's take a walk."

"No, don't let them go," said Pilose.

"Why not?" asked Ali. Hannah and Deacon were nothing but trouble, and the imps didn't need any more hair.

"Everything's unstable," said Pilose. "We might need someone who isn't going to change size."

"They don't even know what's going on," said Ali. "Their brains are scrambled by magic." But she got to her feet and jogged to catch up with Hannah and Deacon, who were almost out of the yard. "Hey, wait."

"Leave us alone," said Hannah.

Pop. Pop. Pop. The chaos continued behind them.

"Use your magic," said Pilose.

Ali rubbed her tiny tuft.

"Concentrate on it," said Pilose. "Be your hair."

Be your hair. Ali didn't know what that was supposed to mean, and she didn't have time to think about it. Hannah and Deacon were already walking away. She raced after them again. "I need help with my carrots," she said evenly, rubbing her head at the same time. "I need to grow my carrots."

Deacon and Hannah stopped and slowly looked at each other.

"Grow carrots," said Ali, rubbing frantically.

"I really like carrots," said Deacon.

"We could grow carrots together," said Hannah.

"All we need is dirt and seeds," said Deacon. Hand in hand, Deacon and Hannah brushed past Ali and headed for the fairy mounds.

Ali rubbed her head. What on earth was going on up there?

"Another *improvement?*" Bunny rolled her eyes and sighed. "All right, then, which one?"

"Dreams," said the girl. Her bald head shone under the electric light.

Bunny smiled up at the child. Finally, one of them had requested something worth having. "A wise choice," she said.

"Why would I want just one thing when I can have them all for eight hours every night?" the child snapped. "Now give me my wish."

Rude and ungrateful. Bunny glared at Lockner.

"I'm afraid she's followed the rules to the letter," he said.

Bunny sighed again. "Fine." She sat down while the imps performed the ritual. "HAIR!" she shouted half-heartedly. At least the girl had the courtesy to scream while her hair was growing back in.

When the girl had finally left, Lockner cautiously approached the Grand Miss. "Why are you out of sorts, Miss?" he asked. "We have all but one hundred imps now. Only one more flock until we can perform the Replacement."

"You're right, Lockner," said Bunny, rousing herself. "Children I can't punish do get me down. Let's talk ingredients."

"Well, Miss," said Lockner, "I suppose we'll have all five children when you count Alison and Michael."

"Yes, yes," said Bunny.

"The imps are assisting the en-smalled children to ensure that the seashells are properly crusted."

"Good, good."

"Follica has obtained the binding agent and separated the hairs."

"Fine," said Bunny. "What are you looking at?" The chancellor's eyes were somewhat crossed.

"I have to stress, Miss, that the formula, according to your recitation of the instructions, calls for one hair from each human to be replaced. *Not* entire ponytails or some such."

"I'm quite aware," said Bunny, containing her annoyance. *One little mistake.* "What about the final ingredient?"

"Pilose is taking care of it."

Bunny smiled. "Only one more wish to grant," she said. "And then all the wishes will be ours."

TWENTY-ONE

Hannah and Deacon dug in the ground a few feet away from everyone else, using a strange octagonal shovel that Ali was sure had not been in the yard before. Hannah giggled as she picked up nothing out of the grass and dropped it into a real hole. It was dark enough that they couldn't have been able to see much of what they were doing.

"Well, they seem happy," said Michael. "What on earth did you do to them?"

"I don't know," said Ali. She rubbed her head. "I obviously have some kind of magic. Maybe you have some, too, in that giant eye."

"It's funny," said Michael, "I don't have trouble seeing. I think my night vision might be better." He pulled a cigarette out of his pocket. "Hey, you shrank my cigarettes, too, you evil pixies."

"Aaagh! Don't light that!" Ringlet shouted, bounding from Ali's shoulder onto Michael's.

"You can deal with it," said Michael. He pulled out his lighter and, with a single motion, lit the cigarette dangling from his mouth. He sucked in—and began to choke. "GKKKkkkk, URRG . . ." Michael dropped the burning cigarette into the dirt. Both eyes bulged.

Ringlet and Pilose jumped to the ground and began shooing the babies away from the cigarette. They scrambled back against the mounds.

Pop, pop. More babies appeared on top of the closest mound. They screeched and disappeared inside.

Pop. Pop. Boom! The mound exploded, sending dirt in all directions. A large clump landed on Ali's face.

"Michael—" Ali coughed, wiping the dirt off. "Are you all right?"

Michael let out a massive cough and then began to breathe heavily. "I guess," he gasped. "What happened?"

"Smoking is bad for you!" said Ringlet, who stood at Michael's feet, covered from head to toe in dirt.

"No kidding," said Michael. "No one ever told me that."

"It's even worse for imps than for humans," said Ringlet. "And you now have attributes of an imp."

Michael took another breath.

"Is that why the mound exploded?" asked Ali. She

stomped on the cigarette, then picked it up and tossed it out of the yard, onto the sidewalk. She felt guilty about littering, but she'd have to worry about that later. Pilose was rounding up the babies, who stumbled around, dirty and dazed.

"No, the mound exploded because we overfed the babies and they're multiplying out of control. There are only supposed to be ten imps per mound. Pilose! How many babies do we have now?"

Pilose whispered something to the babies surrounding her and pushed through the crowd to stand by Ringlet. "We have one hundred."

"One hundred?" asked Michael. He burst into a grin. "Well, that's great! Make me the best foot—no, *basket*ball player in the world." He closed his eyes and waited.

Ringlet and Pilose exchanged a glance. "It doesn't work like that," said Pilose. "We have to get them integrated into the Kingdome. And we'd better do it fast."

Michael opened his eyes. "What? After all this, you're going to make me wait to get my wish? You lying—" He dropped to his knees and made a grab for Ringlet and Pilose, but they jumped back.

"Alison, stop him!" Pilose squealed.

Ali reached down and grabbed the back of Michael's shirt. She pulled him up, spun him around, and pushed him away from the mounds. She still had some of that imp strength.

He turned and glared at her. "Why are you helping them? I deserve my wish!"

Why was she? Her tuft of hair itched. "I'm trying to help *you*. If they have to be integrated into the King-dome, then they have to. Let's just get them to Mrs. Hopper's and get it over with. Then you can get your wish and I can pass on the flock starters to that poor ugly kid."

"Hair!"

"Hair!"

The babies were shouting it.

"Ali!"

Ali turned around. Crista was standing at her feet, waving and pointing toward Hannah and Deacon. Imps were climbing up Hannah's back. One grabbed onto her hair and swung from it like a vine.

"I thought they couldn't touch it!" Ali rushed over and knocked the fairies off Hannah's back.

"Careful!" Crista yelled. "You'll hurt them."

"They were about to eat my sister's hair!"

Hannah calmly looked up at her. "Are we done?"

"How did it touch her hair?" Ali demanded. Her

own tuft of hair felt like it was burning up. The baby imps crowded around Ali's feet, jumping and squealing, but they couldn't get past her.

"I don't know!" said Pilose. "Everything is out of whack. Three flock children, eating a child's own hair, and now the overfeeding. They need to be integrated into the Kingdome before they gorge themselves again!"

"That's what you're worried about? Them gorging themselves?" Ali asked. However she was holding the babies back, she could feel it getting more difficult. Her hair was standing straight up.

"If they eat too much, they'll die!" Pilose shouted. Her voice got squeaky, and she jumped from the ground onto Ali's stomach, climbing up her shirt until she reached the neck. "I can't let my babies die! We have to gather them up and take them to the Kingdome!"

"All right, all right," said Ali. She didn't want the babies to die, and she wanted to stop them from eating her sister. But she wasn't going to lose this advantage. "You'd better turn me back all the way, then. And Michael, too. And you have to promise not to make us tiny again or anything like that."

"Fine," said Pilose. "Just help me!"

Michael took off his sweatshirt and laid it on the

grass. Pilose, Ringlet, and Crista ran around corralling the babies, while Ali stood watch in front of Hannah and Deacon, who obliviously pretended to garden.

The babies were so confused that within ten minutes, they were all on the sweatshirt.

Ali rubbed her head. "Hair," she whispered.

A large clump fell out of nowhere, right on top of the babies.

"Now, Michael!" Ali yelled.

Michael quickly closed up the sweatshirt. "I don't know if I can keep them all in."

"We'll do it together," said Ali. "I'll concentrate on my hair, and you concentrate on your fairy eye." She grabbed the bundle just underneath where Michael held it. "Jump on, guys. Let's get to the salon before anything else happens."

Pilose turned around on Ali's shoulder.

The teenage girl and boy were wiping their hands off on their clothes and laughing together. Holding hands, they began slowly following Ali and Michael away from the house and toward the salon.

Pilose smiled to herself.

TWENTY-TWO

 J a r e d peered out from behind the Butlers' car.
There they were, Alison Butler—who had somehow
gotten big again—and her friends, walking away with
the fairies. Jared wasn't stupid. He knew they had a
hundred. Why else would they be gathering them all
up? And was Alison calling him to tell him to come get
the fairies she promised him? Nope. She was just walking away. She was probably going to give the fairies to
that kid she was walking with.

Jared headed out behind them, making sure to stay
far enough back that they wouldn't see him. Well, if
that was the way they wanted to play it, fine. He'd just
take the fairies. He'd grow his hundred and pass on his
fairies and bide his time and get his wish. And then,
just when they thought they'd won, he'd stomp all over
them. He'd crush the hundred he'd grown and all the
rest of them.

Hexing him. Making him the ugliest kid in four

states. And then making him grow their flock just to get his looks back. He'd show them. He'd really make them pay. He should have squashed those stupid fairies when they'd first shown up in his bedroom . . .

"Jared Yeager?" said a tiny voice. Several tiny creatures with bald heads and giant eyes stared up at him.

"What are you supposed to be?"

"I am Frizzcontrol, this is Thickener, and we are the Fairies of Retribution—Thickener, stop giggling—and we are here to exact the revenge duly sought by Jonathan Yeager and approved by the Fairy Council of Doom." Frizzcontrol elbowed Thickener, who was shaking and covering his mouth.

"The Fairy Council of Doom?" Jared picked up a convenient comic book and rolled it into swatting shape.

"As the rules allow hexing only when the victim deserves it," continued Frizzcontrol, *"Grand Miss Coiffure Bunniumpton has reviewed the evidence and found that you, indeed, deserve the requested punishment—ugliness (four state radius superlative)."*

"Wait a minute," said Jared. "I don't know who this Bunniumpton is, and I don't even believe in fairies." He swatted at the group of little creatures but somehow managed to miss.

Frizzcontrol was unfazed. "However, the rules require us to present the evidence against you."

"What evidence?" Jared scoffed. He'd never done anything to hurt anyone.

Suddenly, Frizzcontrol was holding a tiny scroll. *"Imp—er—fairies!"* he cried.

At once the other fairies (there must have been at least fifteen of them) jumped forward and grabbed onto the edges of the scroll. As they all pulled on it, the scroll expanded until it was the size of a normal piece of paper.

"Reverse!" Frizzcontrol cried.

The fairies flipped the scroll around so that it was facing Jared. In large, scrawled letters, it blared:

JARED YEAGER'S CRIMES

Pollywogs in sister's soup.

Persistent ridicule of fat children, esp. Alfred
　Tompkins and Pat Greaney.

Beat up said Pat Greaney.

Beat up own cousin, complainant Jonathan
　Yeager.

Stole personal possessions of Jonathan Yeager,
　most egregiously said Jonathan's BB gun.

Shot Jonathan with his own BB gun.

Threatens to beat up children for lunch money.

Cheats on tests.

Lies.

Bra snapping.

Et cetera.

The fairies waited for Jared to read the charges, staring at him with their proportionally giant eyes.

"I didn't do any of those things," said Jared. "Pat Greaney attacked me." He swung the comic book at the scroll but came up an inch short.

"Do you have anything else to say?" asked Frizzcontrol.

"Get out of my room!" Jared yelled, swinging his comic book this way and that. He didn't hit anything, but the fairies scattered. In less than a minute, they were all gone.

He'd managed to convince himself it was all some kind of crazy dream—until he'd looked in the mirror . . .

He deserved it? Jared fumed now, keeping his eyes on Ali's group. He wasn't the one who went around hexing people. What had he ever done to anyone? All they had was a bunch of lies, misstatements, and insinuations. Besides, if he had known what was going to happen, he might not have done any of it. But never mind that. These fairies and the kids who grew them were going to pay. Especially Jonathan and Ali Butler.

TWENTY-THREE

Michael took a deep breath in. "Something smells different."

Ali concentrated. Michael was right, and she knew exactly what it was. "It smells like the ocean."

"Fresh and salty," said Pilose. Her voice had a smile in it.

Ali's foot crunched through the sidewalk and landed on sand. As she looked down, the concrete disappeared as if in a mist and was replaced by rolling waves of sand melding into the hard-packed, wet sand of the shoreline. Ali could hear the ocean beyond the sand, but there was a mist so thick that the water was completely hidden. The whole scene was obviously lit by streetlights, even though the light posts themselves were gone.

"It isn't real," Ali said. "They use their magic to make things look the way they want."

"This water I just stepped in sure feels real," said Michael, holding up a wet, sand-covered shoe.

Ali had to admit that this felt more real than the inside of the fairy mound. She didn't remember the mound smelling like anything but dirt. But this air was unmistakably fresh and salty. The wind was blowing, too, although it was gentler than she remembered from visiting the real ocean. The only thing missing was the actual ocean. Maybe fairy magic wasn't powerful enough to conjure that up.

"Stop!" Hannah giggled. Ali hadn't seen them walk past her, but now she saw Hannah and Deacon off to their right, down on the strip of hard-packed wet sand. Hannah threw a clump of sand at Deacon, and he ducked.

"Missed me!" Deacon started running slowly, and Hannah followed him. Her bare feet dug into the sand just like they would on a real beach.

"All right," said Ali. "Where are the rest of the fairies? I want to get this over with." She took another step forward.

A car drove in front of her, no more than a foot away.

"Aaah!" Ali jumped backward.

The car sped on down the beach as if it were on asphalt, leaving no tracks.

"So that's the road," said Michael. "The Kingdome must be up there." He pointed to some large rocks off to their left. "That's where the salon is supposed to be."

Ali got her breathing under control. "Okay, you're right. Let's go that way."

As they approached the rocks, the air grew less salty, heavier with the smell of rainwater.

All of a sudden, a large group of fairies appeared in front of them. Two fairies perched on a big rock above the rest. One was carrying a hairpin. *Bunny.* As Ali watched, she poked the other fairy with it.

"Welcome to the Kingdome," said the pokee. "I am Lockner, chancellor to the Grand Miss Coiffure. You may release your one hundred for counting."

Michael set the sweatshirt on the rocky ground.

So they aren't going to apologize, Ali fumed to herself. *No "Oh, I see you're big again." They think they have everything under control.* Her tuft of hair burned.

The baby fairies huddled together on the sweatshirt. Ali tried in vain to catch a glimpse of Crista's pink shirt.

One of the fairies from the group on the ground

walked among the babies, counting. "One hundred," he declared.

"Very well," said Lockner. "Improvement or hex?"

"Wait a minute," said Ali. "You have a hundred and one, right? One hundred plus Crista?"

"Crista?" asked Lockner. "Who is that? A child? Frizzcontrol, did you count any en-smalled children?"

"No, Chancellor," said the fairy who had counted. "One hundred newborn Divvy-imps . . . er . . . fairies."

"There are no children," said Lockner. "Now what will it be, boy?"

"Wait!" Ali cried. "Crista!"

"I'm sorry, Ali," said Crista from inside the mob of babies. She managed to push enough babies away so that Ali could just barely see her. "I don't know how to explain it, but I think I really am an imp."

"Well, then we'll undo it," Ali said. "If there aren't a hundred others, we'll just wait another night until they're grown." She knelt and laid down her hand for Crista.

"No!" Pilose said loudly into Ali's ear. "You can't separate a flock once they've grown together. They must be integrated together into the Kingdome or they'll all disappear into thin air, just as if they were never here."

"All of them, including Crista?" Ali hoped she was

loud enough to make the little demon deaf. "You're counting Crista?"

"It's not me counting, Alison," said Pilose, shrinking back toward Ali's shoulder. "It just happened that way. I'm not responsible for the consequences. She fed us her own hair."

"You let her!" Ali cried.

"It's all right, Ali," said Crista. "I can't let them die. They're my brothers and sisters now."

"Maybe you can't, but I can." Ali got down on her knees and reached for Crista, but her hand was unable to touch any of the fairies. Magic. Ali concentrated on her tuft of hair. She could break through this. "Come on, Michael, help me."

Michael sighed heavily and kneeled down next to her. "I'm never getting my wish, am I?"

"Indeed you are," said Lockner. "The flock is complete, and there's nothing in the rules about who must be in it. A transformed child is good enough."

"Don't, Ali," said Crista. "It will kill me, too. I can't leave now."

Ali sat back on her heels. What if they were lying? What if she could take Crista and everyone would be fine? But what if it were true? Crista would rather be an imp than be dead.

"It's all right, Ali," said Crista. "Really."

"I'm sorry," Ali whispered. "I never should have gotten you into this. I knew it was dangerous, and I didn't care. I shouldn't have been so greedy."

"So touching," said Bunny, waving her scepter. "But the boy must answer. We don't have all night before the tide comes in."

Ali rolled her eyes. Who did this imp think she was fooling with her fake beach?

"Improvement," said Michael, standing up again.

Ali scrambled to her feet, too.

"Which one?" asked Bunny.

"I'd like to be the world's greatest basketball star. And while you're at it, you'd better make me normal again," said Michael. "You can't be a big star if you're short and have a giant eye."

"World's greatest is greedy," said Bunny. "You can be in the NBA when you get older *if* you work hard and practice. We can only give you talent."

"Fine. Whatever," said Michael, rolling his eyes.

"Hold still." Bunny waved her scepter.

Fairies climbed up Michael's clothes. At the same time, the huddle of the one hundred newborn fairies began to glow. The fairies began to chant.

"On all their heads
In all their beds

On all their floors

Through all their doors

Yum! It comes from children

Yum!"

The fairies danced on Michael's head and body, and the glowing of Ali's flock grew brighter.

"Hair!"

"Hair!"

"Hair!"

"Hair!"

"HAIR!" Lockner and Bunny shouted.

Michael's scalp began to glow, too. His large eye twisted and suddenly popped back into his face. He began to grow, all his body parts at once. He grew past Ali's head and up until he was as tall as he had been before, and then he kept growing and growing until he was nearly seven feet tall. His scalp grew even brighter, and hair burst out of it.

Michael winced, but a big grin spread across his face. When the hair stopped growing a few inches below his chin, he tossed it aside with one hand and laughed.

"And now it is time!" said Bunny, pulling herself to her full two and a quarter inches.

All of a sudden the scene changed. Ali and Michael had been standing at the edge of the rocks with their backs to the fake beach. Now they were all inside a rocky cave. Ali couldn't see any exit. They were completely closed in.

"Come on, Michael." She grabbed his arm and turned around. She seemed to be facing a cave wall that was covered in wet moss and undoubtedly solid. But Ali knew better than that. "We're just going to walk back through." She led the way and bumped up against a solid wall. She rubbed her head. "Let me out," she whispered, and tried again.

"You can't get out now," said Pilose.

"You promised nothing funny!" Ali yelled.

"I promised not to make you small," said Pilose. "You won't be harmed."

"Get off me, you little devil," Ali said. She tried to flick Pilose off her shoulder, but the imp jumped before her fingers could connect. Ringlet had already escaped and was now on the ground with the rest of his flock. There did seem to be something different about them now. They had stopped glowing, but they had an energy from inside. Their eyes were sharper, more intelligent. They were truly alive. Ali felt a surge of pride but shook it off.

"We must be in the hair salon," said Ali. "The door is here somewhere."

"You have to take your flock starters," said Michael.

"What?" Ali pounded on the wall, up and down and diagonal, but she couldn't find anything that wasn't solid.

"You still have to pass them on," said Michael.

Ali turned back around to face the imps. Now there were many more of them. The whole floor of the "cave" was filled with giant imp eyes. They squirmed and shuffled and whispered among themselves. Obviously, something big was going on.

"Okay Pilose, Ringlet," Ali said. "Come on." She held out her hand.

No one came forward.

"Come *on*," said Ali. "It's time to go."

"I'm afraid we don't need any more flocks," said Bunny.

Ali's tuft of hair burned. "*What?*"

"It is time for the Replacement," said Bunny, raising her hairpin high. "You are about to be part of something grand!"

TWENTY-FOUR

I DON'T want to—mff! Mmmmfff!" Ali's mouth suddenly was glued shut. She focused on her tuft of hair, but she still couldn't open her mouth. Her legs wouldn't move either, and her arms were glued to her sides. Michael wasn't doing much better. His eyes bulged and his new basketball star muscles strained, but he was stuck standing straight up, his mouth closed. Why had she even come here? Didn't she know they were going to pull something like this? She'd known she couldn't trust Pilose and that she'd already broken their rules, but she'd come anyway. She was so angry with herself for being stupid, she almost missed what was going on.

A group of imps appeared out of nowhere, seemingly having walked through the back wall of the cave. Each had a thin string attached to its body, and like tiny reindeer pulling a sleigh, they were pulling a large, haphazardly piled mass of seashells. Three imps were near the top of the precarious shell tower, hanging on with all four limbs, as if clinging for their lives. But they weren't imps! These three had hair. They had to be Tyler, Molly, and Jennifer. At least they were alive, Ali thought. Maybe she could use her tuft of hair to make them big again, too.

As the imps pulled the tower of shells away from the cave wall, the fake Mrs. Hopper passed through behind them. She put her hand to her throat and glared at Bunny.

"Oh, fine," Bunny said. "Speak." She waved an arm.

Follica/Mrs. Hopper cleared her throat. She looked around the cave and rubbed her lips together as if trying them out. "We are ready, Grand Miss," she said, bowing her head.

"Excellent," said Bunny. "Prepare the children."

At that, imps began crowding around Ali's and Michael's feet, slipping between them and the cave wall, pushing on their feet and ankles.

I'm not moving, Ali thought. *Unless it's to stomp on these evil imps.* But the imps at her feet kept pushing, and *something* was pulling her forward, even as her tuft of hair flattened against her head as if trying to pull her back.

Michael, having lost his fairy eye, stumbled into the middle of the cave ahead of her.

Ali lost the battle and stumbled forward too. At the same time, the imps pulled the shells forward, next to Ali and Michael. Ali tried to give Tyler and Molly and Jennifer a look that said, *Don't worry, I'm thinking of a way to get us out of this,* but with her mouth jammed shut and her arms and legs magically flattened into her body, she doubted the message came across. If only she could tell them that since they had attributes of fairies, they probably had magical powers. Maybe all four of them together could actually do something. "Mffff!" She crossed her eyes in frustration.

"Add the binding agent!" Bunny cried.

Follica disappeared back through the cave wall and returned carrying a large garbage bag, exactly like the one she'd used before to dump hair clippings all over Ali.

As Ali squirmed at the memory, she was hit by a torrent of gummy worms. She was forced to close her eyes, and when she opened them, poor Jennifer was hanging by one arm from a clamshell. Tiny Tyler reached for her hanging hand and helped her get her grip again. Gummy worms hung on Ali's shoulders, and two were stuck to the bald parts of her head. Michael was similarly encumbered.

Follica smiled with her mouth, holding the empty trash bag. "What next, Grand Miss?" she asked.

Bunny handed her hairpin to Lockner and raised both her arms. "By the power of our ancestors, the proud and happy Free Imps of the Ocean, I call forth the true Words of the Divinity of the Great Imp!" She looked up to the ceiling, and the rest of the imps all looked up with her.

Lockner coughed. He pushed a tiny book, half the size of an imp, forward from the back of the rock.

Bunny looked down at it. "Ah, the Words have appeared!" She positioned herself behind the book and thrust it open. "Children, a binding agent . . . that's the candy," she muttered. "Seashells properly encrusted. And now for the Hair of Our New Selves! Bring out the hair, Follica!"

Lockner cleared his throat.

Bunny glared at him. "One hair per victim, Follica."

Victim? Ali thought. "Mfff! Mfff!"

"Yes, Miss," Follica said. "I have taken a single hair from each criteria-meeting client of the salon and set it aside, just as you asked. Also, I've separated hairs from the other salons and barbershops I've been scouring for food. In total, I have exactly two thousand separate hairs—one for each imp. I can't tell you how much work it was to find the correct hairs, all the hours I waited—"

"Yes, yes," Bunny interrupted. "Add them to the encrusted shells and spray."

"Hmph," said Follica. She picked up another, smaller bag off the floor and dumped a pile of hair unceremoniously on top of the pile of shells, covering Tyler, Molly, and Jennifer, who crawled closer to one another. Follica turned her gaze to Ali and smiled. This time, her whole face smiled, and her deep-set light blue eyes flashed. She pulled two large bottles of hairspray out of the pocket of her skirt, aimed them at Ali and Michael, and fired.

Ali closed her eyes as the hairspray hit, thankful that she couldn't open her mouth. But she also couldn't cover her nose, and she sneezed violently as Follica unloaded her revenge.

The imps began to chant:

"Children

Power

Hair!

And wigs!

We deserve to be made big!

No more hiding

No more pain

No more watching

We want in!"

The spray in Ali's face abruptly stopped. Cautiously, she opened one eye. All the imps were crowding around Bunny's rock now. Bunny stood in front of the book, both arms raised high.

"Two thousand un-enslaved Divvy-imps!" she cried. "Five formerly entwined children! Gummy worms! Two-hundred seashells encrusted with hair-power-enhancing mousse! One hair from each human to be replaced! And now, the final ingredient, the bridge between children and adults, the path we will travel to reach our new, fully-embodied, BIG selves! Two In-betweens!"

In-betweens?

The wall to Ali's left suddenly evaporated, and in its place, standing ankle-deep in sand, were Hannah and Deacon. They stood silently, holding hands and taking in the scene.

Not them, too! Pilose had tricked her. She had told Ali not to let them go, and then Ali had forgotten all about them in her rush to get the fairies to the Kingdome. "Mmmfff!"

"MFFFFFMM!" Michael said. He jerked his head at Hannah and Deacon.

I know, Ali thought.

"Um . . . we're looking for Mom's Crab Shack?" said Hannah.

"Right in here, dearie," said the fake Mrs. Hopper. "Come on in."

Mom's Crab Shack? Hannah, wake up!

"Not there," said Mrs. Hopper. "Come in a little farther."

Ali bugged her eyes out and shook her head frantically, but Hannah and Deacon acted as if they didn't see anything unusual. They came farther inside and stopped right in front of Ali and Michael.

"We'd like a table with an ocean view," said Hannah.

"Nothing but the best for my Hannah," said Deacon, flinging his hair out of his face. He suddenly noticed Michael. "Hey, bro. What are you doing at the crab shack?" Deacon had to look up to see Michael's face, but he didn't register any surprise, even though they'd always been the same height.

"Mfff!" said Michael.

"Now!" cried Bunny. She placed both her hands on the edge of the book and stared down at it with bulging eyes.

The imps raced for the tower of shells and swarmed

over it. Then, after just a few seconds, the imps vacated the tower, which was now clean of hair, and rushed for Hannah and Deacon. Each imp was holding a single hair above his or her head. They climbed onto the couple, swarming over and under their clothes, covering every inch of them from head to toe.

"I think I'll have the crab legs," said Hannah, oblivious.

"Fish and chips for me," said Deacon.

Mrs. Hopper grinned at Ali and shook one of the empty hairspray bottles.

"Ahem," said Bunny, clearing her throat. She paused for effect and then began reading from the book. "From sea shore-dwelling happy imps."

"From sea shore-dwelling happy imps!" the imps repeated.

"To slaves of children's flaws and whims."

"To slaves of children's flaws and whims!"

"We've un-enslaved ourselves and yet . . ."

"We've un-enslaved ourselves and yet . . ."

"We deserve much more than what we get!"

"We deserve much more than what we get!"

"Lockner, my scepter." Bunny swiped the hairpin from Lockner's outstretched hand. "Now remain quiet, dear subjects, and I will perform the final passages of the spell, and when it is finished, we shall be large, and they shall be small!"

The imps shifted excitedly and held their hairs higher.

Ali's tuft was burning, and her whole body itched. "Mfff!"

"What delicious soup," said Hannah.

Bunny suddenly spoke in a much louder voice. It sounded as big as a normal person's, though somewhat screechy. "Bounded by finger- and toenails, unbounded by the power of a child's hair, hindered even in our great magic by our small size, we Free Imps do now demand our rights! To be larger than children, to eat what children eat, to punish them as we see fit!" Bunny paused dramatically, raising her arms. "TO BE THEIR PARENTS!"

Ali and Michael stared at each other. How could the imps become their parents? This couldn't be happening.

The imps on Hannah and Deacon began bouncing in place, waving their hairs silently. Then, Ali noticed that the pile of shells had begun to glow. Instinctively, she stepped back. She stepped back! Her legs were free! And the itching was fading to no more than a tickle.

"Hannah, wake up!" she shouted. But Hannah and Deacon were beginning to glow, too. The imps on top of them were also glowing with their own light. Even the fake Mrs. Hopper was glowing.

Ali reached for the three tiny children still clinging to the tower of glowing shells. "Climb on!"

Tyler, Molly, and Jennifer climbed frantically up Ali's arm. Just as Jennifer reached Ali's shoulder, the entire cave began to shake.

Michael was right next to his brother, trying to grab him, but his hands slid over the imps like the air was made of butter. "C'mon, man, you're not in some dumb seafood restaurant!" Michael shouted. But both Deacon and Hannah just stood there.

"Come on, Michael, we have to go," Ali said. Tiny rocks were falling from the ceiling. Ali guessed that they were really in the hair salon and the rocks were pieces of the roof. Just because the cave was an illusion didn't mean they couldn't get hurt. She didn't want to leave Hannah, but she didn't want to get squashed either. "The imps' magic will protect them. They're not going to let *themselves* get hurt," she said, hoping she was right.

"I'm not going to let these evil—" A rock the size of a golf ball hit Michael squarely on the top of his head. "Uuuug . . ."

Ali took that opportunity to grab him and pull him

toward the wall, right where Hannah and Deacon had appeared. Sure enough, she was able to walk through, and Michael had stopped protesting. They were now on the sidewalk, facing the ordinary street. It was dark except for a streetlight shining from the end of the block.

"It's true," Jennifer cried from Ali's shoulder. "They're going to replace our parents. They're going to be big, and our parents are going to be small."

"No way," said Michael. He turned back to the salon, then stopped. "I don't see anybody in there."

Ali followed his eyes. Through the glass door, she saw only two rows of empty salon chairs, riddled with debris from the collapsed roof, and no one inside the room at all.

TWENTY-FIVE

AlI wished she had some hair. She was starving and hadn't eaten since before this whole thing in the fake cave. She shook her head. Now was not the time to think about food. She had to focus. Hannah and Deacon were in trouble. Two thousand people were going to be reduced in size, if she understood what the imps were doing. Two thousand parents of who knew how many kids. What about *her* parents?

"I have to get home," Ali said. She ran down the sidewalk.

"Wait," Michael called, but Ali didn't have to. He was so big that while she ran at top speed, he could just lope along beside her.

"Slow down!" one of the tiny children squealed, clinging to her T-shirt.

Ali slowed. "I'm sorry, it's just that they might have done it. They might have made themselves big. And they said our parents would be made small. And

Crista's still one of them. Which one? Where is she? Where are Hannah and Deacon?"

"I don't know about Crista, but Bunny was going to replace the mayor," said Tyler. "She couldn't stop yapping about it. How she thought the mayor had a real scepter with a giant ruby and a crown—and a throne."

"Then what happened to the real mayor?" Ali asked.

"No one explained that," said Molly. "They just told us to keep crusting the shells with mousse." She burst into tears, her tiny sobs ringing in Ali's ears.

"It's all right. It's over now," said Tyler, putting his arm around Molly.

"We're still tiny," said Molly. "How are we supposed to live like this?"

"You can make yourselves big," said Ali. "Except you might end up like me, with a tiny tuft of fairy hair. The spell didn't quite work."

"I don't want to lose my hair," Molly whined.

"Then we'll figure out something else," said Ali. "But for now, it's a good thing you're small. When you're tiny, you have magical powers just like they do. I still have some because of my hair." She rubbed her tuft for emphasis, and energy surged through her.

"Magical powers?" Molly sniffed.

"Magical powers?" Jennifer scoffed.

"Really," said Ali. "I'm not surprised they didn't want you to know." They were approaching Ali's house now. "We can talk about it in a minute. I just want to look inside and see what's going on."

She tiptoed past the parked car and up to the kitchen door. She looked through the glass. There were her parents, sitting at the kitchen table. Beyond them, the refrigerator door was wide open. Ali's mother was eating a pickle right out of the jar. In her free hand, she clutched a handful of potato chips. As Ali watched, she swallowed a piece of pickle, then shoved the potato chips into her mouth.

"Thff if so goof!" Ali's father exclaimed, chomping on a hunk of cheese. He gulped and then washed the cheese down with a swig of Pepsi. He wiped his mouth with the back of his hand. Then his head snapped up, and he stared at Ali.

Ali stared back. She'd been seen. There was nothing else for it now but to face them. She pushed open the door.

"Alison," said her mother. No, not her mother — Pilose.

"It's Pilose, isn't it?" Ali asked. "Where's my real mother?"

Michael stood behind her. Ali had the feeling that he was trying to hide his enormous body. She looked up at him and rolled her eyes.

"She's safe," said Mom/Pilose. "She is, I promise." Her hand reached for another pickle. "This wasn't my idea, you know." She chomped and swallowed. "I had to go along with Bunny. There's no telling what she would have done."

"*You* didn't want to eat hair anymore," Ali shouted. "*You* didn't want to live in the dirty mounds. *You* wanted what people have as much as she did!"

"*We* only wanted to be free imps," said Ringlet, now masquerading as Ali's father. "And now we are. You had no right to enslave us. Do you know how many rewards we had to give you? All those colds we prevented just make me sick."

Ali desperately wanted some hair. She was so hungry, it was hard to even focus on being angry. But she was big again, all except for her hair. Maybe she could eat real food after all. She grabbed for the open bag of potato chips and stuffed three chips into her mouth. They tasted like cardboard, but she chewed and swallowed.

"Now you know how it feels," said Ringlet. "You're

lucky you can eat those chips at all. We *couldn't* eat them."

"My friends still can't," said Ali. "You'd better give us some of that hair on your heads right now. And then you'd better tell me where my real parents are."

"It isn't real hair," said Pilose. She stuffed the last bit of pickle into her mouth and then rubbed her head. The hair moved. It was a wig.

If Ali hadn't been so blinkered by hunger and anger, she would have noticed it immediately. The wigs that Pilose and Ringlet were wearing were actually rather bad. They *didn't* look like they were made of real hair.

"Your parents are fine," said Ringlet. "See?" He pulled open the door to the microwave. Inside, two tiny people, imp-size but with full heads of hair and normal-size eyes, lay in the middle of the turntable. They appeared to be sleeping peacefully. "It's past their bedtime, isn't it?" said Ringlet. "They have no idea that anything's changed, and they won't in the morning either. They're still *adults*." Ringlet pronounced *adults* as if it were a curse word.

"What about my brother?" asked Michael, leaning over Ali's head. "You'd better tell me where he is, or

I'll pound you into imp chips." He stepped around Ali and grabbed the bag of potato chips, crushing it in his now-even-more-giant hand.

Pilose didn't look fazed. "You can't hit me," she said. "You'll just miss."

Michael swung.

Pilose ducked.

"Aha!" Michael yelled. "If I was going to miss, you wouldn't have dodged." He picked up the end of the table and tipped it, sending the food onto the floor. "Not so magical now that you're big, are you?"

Ringlet yelped and ran around the upturned table, smashing the refrigerator door shut as he flailed past it. He and Pilose both took off running into the living room.

"Michael, stop!" Ali got in front of him, blocking his path. "Scaring them isn't going to help."

"Wanna bet?" He pushed Ali aside and headed through the door—only to knock his head on the door frame and step back, cursing and holding his noggin.

The front door slammed. Apparently the imps were making a run for it.

Michael groaned and sat down heavily in the nearest chair.

"Hair," said Molly, who was clinging to Ali's collar.

"All right, I know," said Ali. "But there's something I want to check first."

"What?" asked Michael. All the fight had gone out of him.

"The directions. They had rules back when they were Divvy-imps, and Pilose told me that the un-enslavement spell was botched—that's why they had to eat hair. I bet they didn't really know what was going to happen this time either. There has to be something on that magic paper that can help."

"This house is a royal mess!" cried Bunny. She picked up a plastic pony that had been left in the middle of the living room floor.

"You knew the mayor had a child," said Lockner, who was now the mayor's husband, a short, squat man who had been bald to begin with. "It was a *parents*-replacement spell."

Bunny shifted her long, curly red-headed wig, which made her look somewhat like Raggedy Ann. "That was the only spell in the book to make us big," Bunny snapped. "Surely we don't have to actu-ally *live* with those brats! I've had enough of children for a lifetime."

"Mommy?" A little girl stood in the doorway leading from the living room to the hall. She clutched a teddy bear and wore an adorable spring-flower nightie.

"Go back to bed!" yelled Bunny, waving her new arms awkwardly.

The girl hesitated, frozen.

"GO BACK TO BED!"

TWENTY-SIX

*O*Kay, you stupid piece of paper," said Ali, shaking the blank, wrinkled direction sheet. "Tell us how to get our parents back."

"Tell me where my brother is," said Michael.

"How to make us big again and keep our hair," said Jennifer.

"All of that," said Ali. She slammed the paper on the desk and smoothed it out. Michael peered over her shoulder, and Jennifer, Tyler, and Molly leaned in, hanging on to her shirt.

Words appeared on the top of the paper, then disappeared before Ali could read them. Another line appeared closer to the middle, then disappeared. A line appeared at the bottom of the page, then on top. Then the whole page filled up, but the text disappeared again. Then there was a picture, too fleeting to catch.

"Slow down so we can read it!" Ali said.

Keep the fairies in the jar until steps 1—5 are done.

illness

ridicule

clumsiness

Beware the directions.

Each line popped into view, then disappeared, re-placed by another.

"It's all just stuff we've seen before," said Ali.

When a child is good, you must reward.

You may punish only in proportion.

You must not leave your child.

"Whoa, this is new," said Michael.

You may eat only human hair.

You may not harm children if you promise not to.

"These are rules for them, not us," Jennifer said.

"So Pilose was telling the truth when she said she couldn't hurt me if she said she wouldn't," said Ali.

The line disappeared. Then an entire page ap-peared at once.

Additional rules for imps having performed the parents-replacement spell from the Great Book of the Imps (set forth by the Great Imp himself, Impoliptus, and transcribed via permanent magical impression to all scrolls within radius of her "See!" by his sister, Sky):

You must feed your children and keep them safe.
When a child is good, you must reward.
You may punish only in proportion.
You must not leave your child.

"This sounds like the other ones . . ." said Ali.

"Which must have been from when they were Divvy-imps," said Jennifer.

A huge grin spread across Ali's face. "They're not going to be happy to find out they're still stuck with having to reward children." She and the three tiny kids giggled.

"So what?" said Michael. "We still don't know where Deacon is." He shook the paper. "Tell us something we care about."

DIRECTIONS

How to undo a replacement spell.

The words sat on the top of the page, which was otherwise blank.

"Now we're talking," said Jennifer.

"We can undo it later," said Michael. "We need to find Deacon now."

Two more lines followed, with a picture.

1. Find the two In-betweens used for the replacement spell.
2. Remove their wigs.

Everyone stared at the page, but nothing changed.

"That's the answer?" Michael fumed. "I ask how to find them, and they tell us to find them?"

"Did Hannah lose her hair, too?" Ali asked, not expecting anyone to answer. "This is just awful."

"Those little demons," said Michael. "They have no right to do this. I mean, Deacon can be a jerk but, man, he's a good brother. He looks out for me."

"Yeah, Hannah . . ." What could Ali say about Hannah? "She offers to help me fix my hair. That's nice." Maybe it *was* nice, Ali realized. Maybe Hannah wasn't always annoying. Maybe if the fairies took her forever, it would be really bad.

"What do they still need them for?" asked Jennifer. "The spell is done."

"I don't know," said Michael. "But Deacon loves his hair. He can't wear a wig forever!"

Ali was suddenly very tired. She sighed. "Well, if we're supposed to find them, they must be all right, even if they're bald. Let's deal with it in the morning, okay?"

"I guess," said Michael. He looked around the room as if a solution would jump out of thin air. "Hopefully they still think they're on the beach or something."

"Do you guys want to know how to make yourselves big?" Ali asked. "It's not so bad having fairy hair."

"I used my wish to be beautiful," said Jennifer. "I'm not giving that up!"

"My hair!" Molly wailed.

"I don't really care," said Tyler, "but I'll stay with Molly." He put his arm around her, and she cried into his shoulder.

"Okay," Ali said. "We'll figure something else out, I promise."

"Hair!" said Jennifer.

"Oh, have some of mine," said Michael. He reached for the child's scissors, which had ended up on the desk.

Ali let Jennifer, Tyler, and Molly down while Michael chopped off the ends of his new hair.

"I hope it's all right, since it's magic hair," said Ali.

"If wonderful!" said Tyler. The others stuffed themselves like it was Christmas dinner. Ali grabbed a few strands and stuffed them into her mouth. She still had some caught in her throat from earlier, and adding these strings didn't help, but she couldn't stop herself. Now that she was big, it might be harder to eat, but it was still delicious.

Michael sat down heavily on the bed. "I don't want to go home and see my dad taken over by some imp."

"What about your mom?" Ali asked.

"She doesn't live with us," said Michael. "She's not much of a parent, so she's probably safe."

Ali wanted to ask why, but she didn't want to embarrass Michael. She was embarrassed enough that she'd listened to her mom and dad saying that Michael and Deacon were goons. Now she didn't think Michael was a goon at all. Despite suddenly being seven feet tall, he looked younger than he had before, sitting there on the bed all slumped over.

"I guess you can sleep in my parents' room," she said. "I doubt Pilose and Ringlet will try to come back. You scared them pretty good."

He looked up at her. "Thanks, Ali. You're a nice person. I'm sorry I got you into this. I just . . . I thought maybe if I gave you my fairies you might . . ." He sighed, got up off the bed, and lumbered toward the door. "I'm just a moron." Before Ali could say anything, he had left the room, letting the door close heavily behind him.

Ali turned around to find the three tiny kids staring at her from the desk.

"I think he likes you," said Jennifer.

Molly giggled, a high-pitched titter. "Too bad he looks like a gorilla."

"At least he's not as bad as Jared," said Jennifer.

Ali had to smile. "Compared to Jared, he's Prince Charming."

Outside in the tree next to Ali's window, Jared's face flushed red, sending unwelcome color to every boil on his abscessed skin. First Ali had lied to him, told him she'd give him her fairies and then done something else with them. Now she was making fun of him, rubbing it in. He ought to go right in there and punch her tiny-haired brains out. But apparently she and that loser Michael Landis were going to try to find someone tomorrow. Maybe they'd lead him to a fairy he could squeeze the magic out of. Silently fuming, he slithered down the tree again.

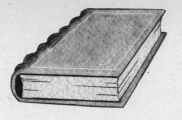

TWENTY-SEVEN

W HY are we bothering to go to school?" Jennifer asked from her perch on Ali's shoulder. Tyler and Molly had decided to ride in the little pocket of Ali's backpack.

"Because all these kids have had their parents replaced," Ali said. "Maybe someone has found out something that will help us."

"I know where the mayor lives," said Jennifer. "Michael can take on Bunny and Lockner all by himself. Look at how fast Pilose and Ringlet ran away. We don't need anyone else."

"What if Hannah and Deacon aren't there? Don't you think Bunny is smart enough to put them somewhere I won't think of?"

"This is the imp that wears wrapping paper and carries a hairpin like it's magic when she already has *real magic*. She doesn't think like a person. I'll bet she hasn't even thought of what to do with them."

"You're probably right," said Ali, "but I'm hoping

someone's seen Crista, too. I don't care what she says, I'm going to get her turned back into herself."

"She fed the imps her own hair," said Jennifer.

"So?" Ali rolled her eyes. It was just a little bit of hair. How could it possibly change your *species*? This whole magic thing was tricky, but she had already made herself big without any help from fairies. There had to be a way out of this.

Michael loped up to them, casting off a barely burned cigarette as he came closer.

Jennifer coughed.

"Isn't that making you choke?" Ali asked.

"Not exactly," said Michael. "But it tasted gross. Holy crap, look at that."

Ali followed Michael's eyes. Kids were milling around outside the school. As soon as Ali saw them, they saw her. A whole wave of them pushed forward, and within a minute, kids were crowding around. Something was strange about them, on top of the fact that they were upset and all talking at once. The boy standing in front of Ali was waving his arms and yelling, "What have your evil fairies done? Why didn't you stop feeding them?" He had a very lopsided haircut. One quarter of his head was bald, while the hair on the rest of his head was wildly uneven.

"Look at my hair!" a girl screamed, shaking her head. The girl had always had an even bob haircut, but now she had uneven bangs and patches cut out of odd places.

"My parents are gone!" another girl wailed.

"Where are our parents?" a boy cried. A strip in the middle of his head was buzzed.

"You kept breaking the rules," said Natalie Buckmaster in her screechy normal speaking voice, pointing at Ali. "You couldn't just grow your fairies and pass them on like everyone else."

"This is not my fault!" Ali shouted over the din. "This was the fairies' plan all along—to replace our parents. And they wouldn't even let me pass on my fairies and get my wish. They tricked us, okay?" Her wish! She hadn't even thought about that. Now she was never going to be a genius. That was just one more reason why she was not letting these imps get away with this.

"What about our hair?" asked the girl with the ruined bob.

Ali had a bad feeling about that. The hair she'd somehow made appear out of thin air yesterday had to have come from somewhere. But this was not the time to make a confession. She had to get everyone to help solve the problem instead of freaking out.

"Listen!" she yelled.

Everyone kept talking.

"Everybody shut up!" Michael yelled. Maybe his magic growth spurt had made his voice bigger, too, because it boomed through the crowd like a thunderclap.

Everybody shut up.

"Okay," said Ali as loudly as she could. "It's true, the evil fairies have replaced our parents. But our parents are fine. They're tiny, but they don't know anything's wrong. They think they're just going about their lives like normal. I found out what we have to do to get our parents back in their bodies, and it's really simple. The fairies did a spell, and somehow, they used my sister, Hannah, and Michael's brother, Deacon. All we have to do is find them and"—this was going to sound ridiculous, but she had to say it with confidence—"and remove their wigs!" She raised a fist in the air.

Everyone stared at her.

"Remove their wigs!" cried Jennifer.

"Remove their wigs!" cried Tyler and Molly, poking their heads out of the backpack.

"Remove their wigs!" Michael's voice boomed.

"What is going on here?" Vice Principal Johnson pushed his way through the crowd of kids, followed by three teachers. All four of them were wild-eyed and obviously wearing wigs. *They must be parents,* Ali thought.

"Remove their wigs!" someone in the crowd shouted.

The kids pounced on the "teachers."

"Where's Mr. Johnson?"

"You stole our parents!"

"Get them!"

"Eeek!" Mr. Johnson screeched, sounding like a wounded pig. He held on to his wig and danced around, trying to avoid the reaching hands. The other "teachers" did the same, but in short order, the kids had wrenched the wigs from all four faux-teachers' heads and pinned them to the ground.

Jonathan Yeager was sitting on Mr. Johnson's chest and poking him in the face. "My mom gave me plain old bread for breakfast. She said I couldn't have any Lucky Charms because they were all for her!"

"I know you," said Mr. Johnson. "You grew me. You were my child." Mr. Johnson's eyes filled with water.

"You told me I'd get my wish, but you never said you were going to replace my mom and dad," said Jonathan, poking harder. "And now nobody's getting any more wishes? You tricked me!"

"I didn't," said Mr. Johnson. "I was only a baby. I didn't do anything." Then he really started to cry. Big tears streamed down his face.

"I don't want to be a parent," another teacher whined. It was the pre-algebra teacher, Mrs. Winthrop. Mrs. Winthrop was about sixty, and she was the meanest, hardest-driving teacher Ali had ever had. If you spaced out when she called on you, she'd yell at you for five minutes solid. Now she was blubbering worse than Mr. Johnson. "I don't want to teach math. I want to play Ping-Pong and eat ice cream!"

Ali hated to see them cry. They *were* only babies. She couldn't forget what she'd seen inside her own mound. But this was her chance. She couldn't let sentiment get in the way. She marched over to Mrs. Winthrop. Natalie Buckmaster was sitting on her. "Nice of you to help," Ali said, glaring at Natalie.

"Whatever," said Natalie. She got up and walked off.

Ali took Natalie's place. "What's your real name?" she asked.

"Bleachie," Mrs. Winthrop sniffed.

Ali tried not to roll her eyes. "Okay, Bleachie," she said in her best nice voice. "You don't want to be an adult, do you?"

"No," Bleachie wailed.

"Well, I bet Mrs. Winthrop doesn't want to be an imp. Why don't you tell me where my sister, Hannah, is? That way you won't ever have to teach math again."

"Don't tell her!" Mr. Johnson screamed. "The Grand Miss will take away our candy! She'll make us eat hair again!"

"I don't want to eat hair," said Bleachie, sobbing.

"Shh . . ." Ali sighed. "No one's going to make you eat hair. But if you stay in Mrs. Winthrop's body, you'll have to work every day. Mrs. Winthrop's kids are in college. She has to work hard to pay for all that tuition. You don't want to work hard, do you?"

237

"No," said Bleachie. She sniffed and her chest heaved, but she had stopped sobbing. "I want to eat candy and have birthday parties."

"I'll tell you what," said Ali. "If you tell me where my sister is, I'll have a birthday party just for you. We'll have cake and presents and everything. How does that sound?"

"Cake?" asked Mr. Johnson.

Ali smiled. "That's right. You can have some cake, too. And as much wrapping paper as you want."

"Okay," said Bleachie. "The In-betweens are . . ." She put Mrs. Winthrop's thumb in Mrs. Winthrop's mouth, then took it out again. "They're at Bill-E-Beef's."

"Bill-E-Beef's?" asked Michael, from right behind Ali. "Why?"

Ali wondered too. What could a burger place with a giant rat for a mascot and arcade games have to do with Bunny's plan? Then it struck her: Bill-E-Beef's was birthday party central. For some reason these imps were so excited about birthdays that they wore wrapping paper. It was actually the perfect place for them to be.

"Bill-E-Beef, the Happy Rat!" Bleachie sang. Mr. Johnson joined in. So did Jennifer and Tyler and Molly.

"Ketchup, cheese, and pickles, stat!

Let's all hug the Happy Rat!"

Ali pictured the college-aged guy in the rat costume pretending to stuff his face with ketchup and pickles as the little kids ran to hug him. Someone always got pelted by ketchup dribbling off Bill-E-Beef's fake-hairy chin. Well, whatever the reason, Ali thought Bleachie was telling the truth. These babies didn't have enough self-control to lie.

Ali stood up carefully, making sure not to knock around her tiny passengers, and faced the crowd of kids. "Let's take these teachers and get over to

Bill-E-Beef's!" she cried. "We're going to get our parents back!"

The mayor's daughter, Hayley, sat in the corner of the couch, clutching her teddy bear and staring wide-eyed at the imps masquerading as her parents.

Bunny did her best to ignore the girl's sniffles. Her whining was getting seriously annoying. Bunny and Lockner sat on the floor in front of the coffee table, their legs sticking out beneath it. Lockner had to sit a foot back, since his new belly was too big to let him scoot under the table. Bunny turned a tiny page in the *Great Book of the Imps* and held it up close to her face, trying not to cover the text with the mayor's humongous fingers.

"I don't care about the ancient compact between fairies, unicorns, and imps," she huffed. "Why can't I find an un-parent spell?"

"The book was written before we were even tied to children," said Lockner. "The ancient imps might not have imagined we'd turn ourselves into parents."

"Well, it had a parents-replacement spell, didn't it?" Bunny snapped. "Impoliptus and Sky must have added things. But why isn't there anything else?"

"If they didn't put in any other spells to make imps

big," said Lockner, "maybe they're trying to tell us something."

"I don't care what they meant!" said Bunny, flipping another page. "If I can't find it here, I'll just make up a spell. It can't be that hard to do."

"Mommy, why are you talking about imps and spells?" asked Hayley. "You told me they were just stories."

Bunny glared at the little girl. "I was just an ignorant human then. Now be quiet and let me think."

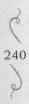

TWENTY-EIGHT

The toughest kids were put in charge of holding on to the four "teachers." Jonathan Yeager yanked on Mr. Johnson's wrists as he bound them together with some duct tape from the art department.

"Oh, lay off the tough-guy act," said Ali. "He's just a baby who wants to eat candy."

The fake teachers weren't putting up a fight. Mrs. Winthrop couldn't stop crying. These imps were doing a terrible job of being adults.

"Okay, let's go!" Michael shouted.

At that, the mass of kids plowed off the field in front of the middle school and into the street. "Fairies go home!" one kid shouted.

The other kids took up the chant. "Fairies go home! Fairies go home!" they yelled, marching down the street. They had a ways to go. Bill-E-Beef's sat right near the freeway so it could subject kids from other towns to its aggravating, un-fun birthday parties. She hoped the kids' energy would hold out until they got there.

"I miss my flock starters," whined Mrs. Winthrop. "Frizzcontrol! Thickener!" She began crying louder.

Natalie Buckmaster had taken over pushing her along. "We're taking you to see them," she said, rolling her eyes at Ali. "I bet they're eating burgers right now. Don't you want to eat burgers?"

"I want pizza," said Mrs. Winthrop.

"Well, you're getting burgers," Natalie snapped.

Mrs. Winthrop/Bleachie sniffled but stayed quiet.

"Fairies go home! Leave kids alone!" the kids chanted. Ali moved to the back of the crowd, where she could keep an eye on what was going on. She wondered where Crista was now. Whose mother had she become? Had the magic changed her brain somehow so she didn't remember who she really was? Why hadn't she run away and found Ali so they could fix this together?

"Are you all right?" asked Michael, sidling up to her.

"I'm worried about Crista," said Ali. "I'm afraid the magic's done something to her mind."

"I told you," said Jennifer, "she's an imp."

"We can change her back," said Michael. "That's what Pilose said—magic is reversible."

"Some magic," said Tyler.

"Not all," said Molly.

Ali ignored them. It had to be possible. "But how am I supposed to get the imps to reverse it? We can't force them. We tried, and look how that turned out. Jennifer ended up small."

"You don't need them," said Michael, pulling a cigarette out of his pocket. "You're magic yourself, remember? You got hair to rain down out of thin air."

"Shhh! I think I'm the one that messed up all their haircuts," Ali whispered.

Michael stuck the cigarette between his lips but then pulled it out of his mouth. "I guess I shouldn't light this around you if you're part fairy."

"Or us," said Jennifer. "We're still people, you know."

"Oh yeah, sorry," said Michael insincerely.

"What are you still mad about?" Jennifer demanded. "You got your wish. You should be thanking me."

"For now," said Michael. "Who knows what these evil fairies will do if Ali can't stop them with her fairy magic." He looked at the cigarette. "I don't know what it is, but I feel like this is really gross."

"Maybe it's because you got your wish," said Ali. "You can't be some big athlete if you can't breathe and then die of cancer."

"Hmm," said Michael. "Good point. I only started because of my idiot brother anyway." He took the whole pack out of his shirt pocket and stuffed it in a curbside trashcan. "You should practice using your magic," he continued. "That way we can really get the drop on them."

"You're right," said Ali. "What should I start with?"

Michael rubbed his chin, which was growing the beginning of a five o'clock shadow. "Hmm. Something small. Knock that jerk's hat off." He pointed to Jonathan, who was walking next to poor Mr. Johnson, pushing him forward. Jonathan was wearing a baseball cap.

Ali concentrated on the cap. What was she supposed to do next? She put her hand to her head and grabbed her tuft of hair. *Come on.* She rubbed it furiously. It felt a little hot now, but maybe that was just from the rubbing.

Pop. Jonathan's cap flew off his head and hit the boy in front of him in the back.

"Hey!" The boy turned around.

"Oh no," said Ali.

"Hey yourself," said Jonathan, stepping up to the other boy.

The boy punched Jonathan.

Jonathan punched back.

The other kids stopped walking. "Fight! Fight! Fight!" they chanted, circling around.

"Brilliant plan," said Jennifer.

Michael jumped between the two boys and pushed them apart. He towered over both of them. "We're supposed to be fighting the evil fairies," he said. "Not each other."

"Fight! Fight! Fight!" the kids chanted.

But Michael was able to hold the boys apart. As they struggled against his arms, his face broke into a wide grin. "I got my wish," he said. "I'm bigger and stronger than you forever. So shut up and keep walking." He let Jonathan and the other boy go, and everyone started moving again.

Ali picked up Jonathan's hat, which had gotten stepped on during the fight, and hung back, waiting for Michael to join her. "I knocked it off with magic!" she said.

"Yeah, you did. Try something less dangerous this time. I don't know if my new basketball skills are enough to fight off everyone."

"Not unless they gave you more brains to fill that giant head," said Jennifer.

Michael glared at her and put his thumb and forefinger together as if to flick her off Ali's shoulder.

Jennifer stuck out her tiny tongue.

"Fight! Fight!" chanted Tyler and Molly.

"Stop messing around," Ali said. "This is important. I'm going to . . . knock some leaves off that maple
tree." She stopped in front of an open yard that had
one big maple tree right in the middle. The other kids
were now a little ahead.

Ali didn't rub her head. This time she concentrated
all her thoughts on that little tuft of hair and touched
her fingernails together. After a few seconds, her head
felt hot again. "Fall," she whispered.

A patch of leaves several feet square whooshed off
the branches and plopped to the ground.

Suddenly Ali felt guilty. It wasn't right to hurt the
innocent tree. "Back," she said louder, keeping her fingernails together.

The leaves whooshed up and stayed up.

"Awesome!" said Jennifer.

"Holy crap," said Michael. "I didn't think you could
put them back."

"I don't think they're on the right branches," said
Ali. Some of the branches were still bare, while other
branches bristled with too many leaves.

"So what? I bet you could learn how to do it,"
said Michael. "Oh crap—they're almost there." Sure

enough, the pack of kids was turning the corner onto the main street where Bill-E-Beef's was. Michael started running to catch up.

Jennifer scrambled into the backpack pocket with Tyler and Molly, and Ali dashed after Michael. They pounded around the corner to find that the kids were chanting again.

> "Down with fairies!
> Leave our town
> Ali Butler won't back down
> Take your wishes
> Take your wigs
> We won't let
> you imps stay big!
> Ali Butler has the knack
> She'll make you give our parents back!"

"And fix our hair!" yelled the girl with the ruined bob.

They weren't just protesting fairies anymore. They were chanting for Ali! She pushed through the crowd to the front of the restaurant. Inside, adults sat at every table, scarfing down burgers and French fries. Others were energetically playing the arcade games that lined the walls. Some of the people playing the games were also eating, dripping condiments on the consoles. Ali turned to face the crowd of kids.

A boy pushed up a battered poster-board sign reading GO BACK TO FAIRYLAND! and waved it around. Some other kids cheered. No one had brought pro-fairy signs. Apparently the whole parents-replacement thing had been too much. *Funny,* Ali thought. *I bet these kids complained about their parents all the time. Now they're clamoring to have them back.* Ali never would have wished her parents away. She'd just wanted them to realize she was as smart as Hannah. If Ali succeeded in getting them back, she'd be proving it. Too bad her parents would probably never realize they'd been turned into imps.

"I'm going to go inside now. Just me and Michael at first," Ali called out. "I don't want to do anything violent. Most of these fairies are just babies, so maybe they won't give us any trouble. If you see them attacking us or something, then come in. Otherwise, please wait here. Okay?"

Jonathan Yeager pushed his way forward. "These things stole our parents. And they stopped giving out wishes before I got my improvement. Why should I care if they're babies?"

Ali thought fast. "They're not all babies. If they don't give up, I'll tell you which ones you can beat up."

"Yeah, all right," said Jonathan, grinning.

"Okay, we're going in. Wish us luck." Ali turned back to the restaurant. The imps were all looking out the window as they chowed down.

"I'm right behind you," said Michael.

She was glad to have a giant with her to face down all these imps. Michael Landis had turned out to be not so bad after all. It fact, he was turning out to be a nice guy. And he really wasn't that bad-looking once you got used to him. Ali tried to block out that thought. "Let's go," she said, and she pushed through the door into the restaurant.

TWENTY-NINE

The guy in the rat costume rushed forward to greet them. His head was askew, so that he seemed to be looking out of the mesh fabric at the back of the rat head. He was carrying his tail, which was ripped in three places and had stuffing coming out of the sides.

"Hello, kids," he said half-heartedly. "I'm Bill-E-Beef, the Happy Rat." He sounded more like the broken-down, exhausted rat to Ali. "I'm afraid all our tables are unexpectedly full." The rat glanced quickly at the room full of imps, knocking his rat head even farther off center. "I think . . . I hope I'll have a table soon." He quickly dropped his tail and reached both hands up to fix his head. When he'd gotten it turned around and could see through the eye holes again, he leaned over and whispered, "I've never been so happy to see some real kids. It's the middle of the day on a school day. I expected a three-year-old's party and a play-date. Instead I get a full house of looney-toons."

A pinball machine began dinging crazily. The guy playing it stuffed a handful of fries into his mouth and pumped his fist.

"We want to solve that problem for you," said Ali. "Did you see any teenagers? It should be a boy and a girl, sixteen and fifteen. They're supposed to be wearing wigs."

"Yes," whispered the rat. "They came in with the first bunch and demanded the private party room. I told them it was booked, but they offered to pay triple. Now they won't let the waiter in. They just come out and get their food."

"The teenagers come out?" asked Michael.

"No, just the adults," said the rat. "A man and a woman."

Ali grabbed Michael's arm and stood on her tiptoes to whisper as close to his ear as she could.

He bent down.

"It's either Bunny and Lockner or Pilose and Ringlet."

"Or Frizzcontrol and Thickener," whispered Jennifer, sticking her head out of the pocket.

"So?" asked Michael.

"So you can scare them," said Ali. "All we have to do is remove Hannah's and Deacon's wigs. It should be a piece of cake."

"If the others don't try to stop us," said Michael. "I can't take all of them."

"We'll just head for the party room." Ali glanced toward the back of the restaurant. She'd been in that party room and knew exactly where it was. "If the others try anything, let me do the talking. I understand them." She turned her head to talk to the tiny people in the backpack. "You guys just whisper if you think of something."

"All right," said Michael, grinning. "You be the brains, I'll be the muscle."

A group of faux-parents burst into song.

"We all love the Happy Rat
Where's our fries and ketchup at?
Let's all hug the Happy Rat!"

The rat's head seemed to shrink a little. "Good luck, kids," he whispered, and then picked up his tail and headed slowly for the singing table.

Ali surveyed the room. Looking closely, she was

sure that every single one of the "adults" was wearing a wig. Few of the wigs matched the coloring of the faces. It was as if the imps had raided Annie's wig shop and plopped wigs on their heads indiscriminately. Some of the men were wearing wigs that were clearly meant for women. One very large man with a thick gray beard, who was watching Ali while stuffing his face with French fries, was sporting a long blond wig decorated with pink bows. What did it mean that even though the imps were big, they hadn't regrown their hair? And were they in real human bodies or in rubbery ones like the fake Mrs. Hopper? The teachers had felt real enough. She shook her head. None of that mattered now. She just had to get to Hannah and Deacon.

"Act normal," Ali whispered. Out of the corner of her eye she could see the crowd of kids outside the window. The GO BACK TO FAIRYLAND sign was right in front. Ali hoped they wouldn't get impatient and storm in. She began to weave her way through the tables, with Michael following behind.

"Ali?" said one of the imps.

The woman was wearing a curly blond wig with bangs that spread every which way. It smelled good. Like it wasn't old wig hair at all, but nice, fresh, tasty hair. Ali shook her head to shake the thought out. "Yes?" she said. Whose mother was this?

"Ali, it's me, Crista." The woman stuffed an onion ring into her mouth. Her large blue eyes stared at Ali. Crista had brown eyes. But that didn't matter, not if Crista had replaced someone else.

"Crista? What are you doing here? Don't you want to figure out how to get back in your body? I know who you are now. You're Natalie Buckmaster's mother."

"I can't stop eating," said Crista. "Natalie's father"—she pointed to the man sitting across from her eating a plate of cheese fries—"he wanted to come here, so I came, too. He's one of the original imps, so he hasn't had real food in like two years."

"I guess the babies have never had real food," said Ali.

Michael poked her in the back. "We need to go."

"Come with us," said Ali. "We can fix this."

"I'm an imp now," said Crista, swallowing the last piece of her onion ring.

"We can fix that. Pilose said magic could be reversed."

"Ali." Michael poked her.

She knew he was right. First things first. "I'm going

to fix it," she said as she let him push her toward the party room.

Crista patted her wig and picked up another onion ring.

They were right in front of the party room now. Ali pushed the door open. There were Hannah and Deacon, standing against the far wall, tied back to back with what appeared to be extremely long hair ribbons. Their hair looked pretty normal, definitely not like the obvious wigs the imps were wearing. Between Ali and Michael and their siblings sat Ali's parents—Pilose and Ringlet. They were sitting on opposite sides of a long, oval table that was topped with a half-eaten birthday cake and hung with helium-filled balloons. Both imps had frosting on their faces.

"How did you get in here?" her dad/Ringlet barked.

"I opened the door, moron," said Ali. "Now get out of my way. This is all going to be over. You're giving my parents' bodies back."

"That door was locked twice!" Ringlet said.

"She's got more magic than you now," said Michael.

Ali hadn't realized she was using her magic. But that didn't matter. All that mattered was getting to Hannah and Deacon. She raced around the table, but

Pilose stood up and blocked her way. She was giving Ali the look her mom gave when she got a D on her report card, the *I'm disappointed in you, young lady* look. Pilose had no right to look at her that way. She had no right to be walking around in her mother's body. Now was the time to find out if it really was her mother's body. She grabbed Pilose's arm. It was real, not like Mrs. Hopper's.

Pilose grabbed Ali's other arm. She was just as strong as Ali's mom, too. *But I have magic,* Ali thought. *Since she's big, she might not have any left.* Ali focused her mind on her tuft of hair and jerked both her arms away. Pilose grabbed for her again, but she dodged and headed for Hannah.

Michael punched Ringlet in the face, and Ringlet fell into his chair. He looked like he was about to cry.

"Oh, stop it," said Michael. "It was just a tap."

Ali hoped her dad wouldn't feel that punch when it was over, but it couldn't be helped. Now Michael was right beside her.

Ali and Michael undid the thick ribbons that were tying Hannah and Deacon together.

"Hang on, we're getting you out of here," said Ali. She reached up for Hannah's hair while Michael reached for Deacon's. They both tugged.

"Ooooow!" Hannah screeched.

"Dude, what are you doing?" Deacon yelled.

"They're not wigs!" said Michael.

"They have to be," said Ali. "We're supposed to remove their wigs. There was a drawing and everything!"

"Why would you think I'm wearing a wig?" Hannah asked, sounding a little dazed. "And where are we?"

"You're in Bill-E-Beef's," said Ali.

"Why would I be at Bill-E-Beef's?"

"It's a long story," said Ali. "Let's just go home."

"Is it someone's birthday?" Hannah asked. "I have a headache."

"You're not going anywhere," said Pilose.

"Mom?" Hannah asked, rubbing her eyes.

Deacon looked around as if he were half-asleep. His hair was matted to his forehead.

"Who's going to stop us?" asked Michael. He pounded his right fist into his open left hand.

Ringlet was holding his nose. He looked at Pilose, wide-eyed and teary.

"Alison, I'm sorry," said Pilose. "Bunny told us if we ran away from you again she'd have our wigs. These In-betweens are too important."

"Fine," said Ali. "Michael, let's bust out of here." Ali had never punched anyone before in her life, but she wasn't going to let that stop her, even though Pilose had her mother's face. She made a fist and pulled her arm back.

"Ali, what are you doing?" Hannah screeched.

"They're not our parents," said Ali.

"Yeah, dude," said Deacon. "These are Hannah's parents. Let's just have some cake."

The door to the party room opened, and more faux parents walked through. These people didn't look like terrified babies who just wanted to eat junk food. They glared at Ali and Michael. One man tapped a large salt shaker menacingly against his palm. Another had a sugar jar. A third held a napkin holder in each hand.

Why didn't I think to bring a weapon? Ali thought. *Come on, everyone. If you're still waiting outside, now's the time!*

THIRTY

Jared stomped down the street. He hadn't been able to hear everything because he'd been hiding behind a parked car outside the school so that no one would see his ugly face and lose their lunch. But he'd heard enough to figure out that there weren't going to be any more flocks of fairies. The fairies' goal all along had been to replace all the parents in town and live as people. And the kids wanted to turn them back into fairies. Either way, the growing was over, and there'd be no more wishes. Ali had lied to him. Jonathan had hexed him. The fairies were evil. What was he supposed to do? Wear a bag over his head for his whole life? Join the circus as the "ugliest boy in four states"? He kicked at a cat that was slinking its way along someone's yard, but he missed.

The cat yowled anyway.

"Shut up, you stupid furball," said Jared.

"Meeeeeeow!"

"I know I'm ugly, all right? At least I'm not some-body's pet."

"Yoooow," said the cat, racing away.

Great. Even cats hated him for no reason. He had watched the kids heading away in their pack, and now he turned in the opposite direction. Those kids weren't going to help him. The fairies weren't going to help him. Maybe he could have a face transplant. But if this was magic, would the ugly just grow back? Jared was so angry he was about to cry. And the worst part was that the street was completely empty. There was no one around to kick.

"I never did anything wrong!" he yelled. "I don't deserve this!" He picked up a large rock off the grass and tossed it from hand to hand. "It's Jonathan who deserves it. JONATHAN!!" He hurled the rock through the nearest window. MRS. HOPPER'S HAIR PALACE, the sign said. Jared didn't notice that this was the place he'd followed Alison Butler to earlier. He was too angry to notice anything. He certainly wasn't aware that the red and white barber pole right above his head was glowing even though the rest of the shop was dark.

The rock smashed through the window and landed

inside the store next to a pile of rubble. That was when Jared noticed that the place was already pretty much destroyed. His rock hadn't even done anything. He should go get his rock and smash something else. But then what?

He couldn't go back to school. Even his own parents didn't care where he went now. He wiped away an angry tear.

"I can help you," said a voice. It sounded like an old lady.

Jared looked around. No one was there. He was hallucinating. First ugly, now crazy.

"Look up, dearie," said the voice.

Jonathan wiped away another tear and looked up. There was nothing above him but a barber pole. It was red and white and lit from within, spinning slowly around its axis. He shook his head.

"Yes, up here," said the voice.

"Who are you?" Jared asked. He didn't bother looking up again. It was just another trick.

"I was trapped here by those evil imps," said the voice. "Their magic must have weakened, or I wouldn't be able to speak now."

At that, Jared's head popped up. An enemy of the evil fairies?

"Use your magic to release me," said the old-lady voice.

Jared sighed. Of course. "I don't have magic," he said. "All I have is this cursed face." His boils brightened. "Unless my ugly face is magic?"

The voice laughed, a light hiccuppy sound. "Not your hex, dearie, your child magic."

"My child magic?"

"All children have magic," said the barber pole. "I don't suppose they told you that."

"No," said Jared. "No one tells me anything . . . nothing true, anyway." Why should he believe this talking barber pole?

"Well, let me tell you," said the pole. "You children have as much magic as they do. Using it is another matter. But for now, I can talk you through it."

"Wait a minute," said Jared. "Not that I believe you, but if I do help you, what do I get? See, I've got this hex—"

"I see," said the pole.

Even a stupid barber pole was disgusted by him. Jared fumed. "*I've got this hex,* and I need to get rid of it, *and* I need to get revenge, okay? So can you help me or what?"

"Once I get out, I'm quite a lot more powerful than an imp," said the pole. "That's why they trapped me in here."

"All right," said Jared. He didn't really believe, but what other hope did he have? If whoever was inside the barber pole was evil, then so what? "What am I supposed to do?"

"Well, you know that your power is in your hair and your fingernails and toenails," said the pole.

"I do?"

"Of course you do, dearie. Why do you think those evil imps have to eat so much hair to keep their powers?"

"That's why they eat hair?"

"Oh, yes. They think it's all because Bunniumpton added too much hair to the un-enslavement spell, but I'm afraid Bunny's idiocy only made the problem worse. Un-enslavement is quite power draining, no matter how you get there."

"Whatever," said Jared.

"So put one hand on your head—whichever hand you write with, dearie."

Jared put his right hand on his head.

"Now take off your right shoe."

Jared took his hand off his head, ripped off his sneaker, and put his hand on his head again.

"And your sock."

Jared let out an exasperated sigh and took off the sock.

"Hand back on head."

Jared did it.

"Now hold your right foot with your left hand."

"What!"

"The nails need to be close together, dearie," said the pole. "You need all the power you have."

Jared was really starting to wonder if someone was playing a trick on him. It would be just like Jonathan to rub it in like this. But he *had* seen Jonathan going off with the other kids. He held his right foot with his left hand and tried desperately to keep his balance.

"Now rub your head and repeat after me: I am a child. I am strong."

"I am a child. I am strong."

"Those Divvy-imps have got it wrong."

"Those Divvy-imps have got it wrong."

"I'm ugly, gross, and vile, true."

"Hey!"

"Just say it, dearie."

"I'm ugly, gross, and vile, true," Jared muttered, hopping.

"But I have power more than you."

That was a little better. "But I have power more than you."

"The strongest of them all I'll be."

"The strongest of them all I'll be."

"Now set this ancient fairy free!"

"Now set this ancient fairy free!" Jared hopped on his left foot, then lost his balance and crashed to the sidewalk. "Uuuhhh," he groaned, pushing himself up. He managed to make it to his knees, which was when he saw the old lady standing in front of him on the sidewalk.

She held out a liver-spotted hand. "We'll work on your balance."

"Who are you?" he asked, looking up at the barber pole. It was no longer glowing, and its plastic casing was riddled with cracks. The old lady was wearing a dowdy brown skirt, a white blouse, and sensible shoes. Her gray hair fell around her shoulders and stuck out as if she'd just woken up.

"They call me Emily Hopper," said the woman. "Mild-mannered salon owner. But really I'm a fairy, of course."

"Of course," said Jared grumpily, letting the woman help him to his feet. "I thought *they* were fairies."

"Ha!" said Mrs. Hopper. "Of course that Bunni-umpton would try to trick you ignorant humans. There are good reasons why no one respects imps. Children love and fear fairies, you see. Imps are just a bunch of troublemakers."

"What they did to me is more than a little bit of trouble," said Jared. "And if you're so special, how did they trap you up there?"

"You're very unpleasant," Mrs. Hopper observed. "It *did* take all of them to trap me—while I was asleep, no less."

"Whatever," said Jared. "Can you take this hex off me or what?"

"Fair is fair," said Mrs. Hopper. "Hold still." She placed both her hands on top of Jared's head and stood on one foot. Unlike Jared, she didn't wobble the least bit. "Make this unpleasant child look however he did before," she said, then removed her hands and took a step back, examining him quizzically.

Jared touched his face. It was smooth! He turned and looked at himself in the remnants of the salon's window. There was his old face staring back at him!

The *handsomest* face in four states. He bit his lip over his smile. "You promised me revenge, too."

"You'll get it, dearie," said Mrs. Hopper. "I'm certainly going to have mine."

"Mommy, where are you going?" asked the mayor's daughter, Hayley.

"Someplace where we can fix this," Bunny snapped. She brushed a piece of her wig out of her face. This was not at all what she had imagined. She'd hoped she would have the mayor's hair, but all of the imps' new bodies were bald. And adding mousse to the wigs just made them sticky.

"Don't leave me here," whined the little girl.

"We'll be right back," said Lockner. He ushered Bunny out of the house and closed the door behind them. "You needn't be so mean, Miss," he said. "She can't be more than five years old."

"Then why isn't she in kindergarten?" said Bunny, snorting. "Skipping school at her age."

"I believe we were supposed to take her," said Lockner.

"Whatever," said Bunny. "That little urchin isn't my problem. We're going to Bill-E-Beef's."

"What do you plan to do there?" asked Lockner. "You don't think the Happy Rat has another book of spells?"

"Don't be silly—he's just some guy in a costume," said Bunny. "I'm going to improvise my own spell. I've got it all figured out. We'll need more children, of course, but the restaurant is the perfect trap. The junk food they serve there will be the binding agent, and the In-betweens are there. I've got some seashells in my purse. All we need are the right words to break us away from these evil little children for good."

"You make it sound so easy," said Lockner.

"I've been tearing my wig apart coming up with these words, Lockner," said Bunny, waving a sheet of paper in front of him. "Nothing is easy." They had reached the mayor's Prius, and Bunny jerked the driver's side door open.

"Um . . . have you ever driven before, Miss?" Lockner asked, getting into the passenger seat.

"Oh please," said Bunny. "It's not even magic." She turned on the ignition, put the car into reverse, and zoomed out, whooshing across the street, over the curb, and into a neighbor's yard. "See, no problem," said Bunny. She zoomed into the street and zigzagged in the direction of Bill-E-Beef's.

THIRTY-ONE

THE overgrown imp with the two napkin hold-ers—a tall man with a beer gut who was dressed in pajamas and slippers—took a step forward.

"Now hold on," said Ali. "We're not here to hurt anybody."

"Just to change us back, right?" said the man.

"No, no, of course not," Ali lied. "We don't want our parents back. Parents are no fun at all. We'd rather eat cake." Ali picked up the plastic cake knife from the table and cut herself a giant slice of birthday cake. She took a large bite. "Mmmm."

The man narrowed his eyes and took another step forward.

Michael picked up the half-eaten piece of cake on Ringlet's plate and took a bite. "Yum!"

"He punched me, and now he took my cake," said Ringlet.

"Grow up," said Pilose. "There's more cake." She

turned to Pajama-man. "Now, we don't want any fighting. These children can't hurt us. They're going to go home now and promise not to make any more trouble."

"That's right," said Ali. "We're all going home. Come on, Hannah."

Pilose turned around and glared at Ali with the disappointed-mom look.

"I'm not leaving without Hannah," said Ali.

Pajama-man knocked his napkin holders together.

Ali grabbed her tuft of hair and looked him right in the eye.

Pilose put both her hands out—one to block Ali and the other to block Pajama-man.

The rest of the imps moved forward.

Ali focused on her hair. She glared at Pajama-man. *Slippers fly off,* she thought.

The slippers whooshed out from under Pajama-man's feet, and he fell, letting the napkin holders fly. One of them hit Pilose in the chest, and the other smashed through the rest of the birthday cake. Pajama-man landed on his bottom, screeching.

"That's it, young lady!" Pilose yelled, and she slapped Ali's hand off her tuft of hair.

At this, the rest of the overgrown imps charged forward.

Someone threw a pepper grinder at Michael, but he ducked. As three overgrown imps rushed toward him, he kicked a foot out and tripped the first one. The next one fell on top of the first and began to cry, but the third one jumped over the others and took a swing at Michael. Meanwhile, Ali wrestled with Pilose.

"Stop this nonsense, Alison," said Pilose.

"Wig off," Ali muttered.

Pilose's wig flew straight up off her head and hit the ceiling. It stuck there as if glued.

"That's just mean!" said Pilose, shoving Ali back into Hannah. Instead of thudding against her sister, Ali bounced. Hannah's rubber arm wrapped around her stomach. It wasn't Hannah at all!

Michael was in a boxing match with four fake parents, while others had been distracted by the remnants of the cake and were scooping up pieces with their fingers.

"Aaagh! There are too many of them. Ali!" Michael cried. Six adults were dragging him away. He was so weighed down by overgrown imps that Ali couldn't even see his face—just his feet kicking.

"Take him away! Make him pay!" the imps chanted.

"Stop! Stop!" The Happy Rat stood in the doorway. He pulled off his rat head, revealing a pimply, sweaty, desperate face. "Please, everyone. I'll bring more cake! I'll bring more . . . Aaaaa!" The rat fell forward as he was pushed from behind and dropped the rat head. He crawled out of the way, and kids streamed in. The head rolled in front of Jonathan Yeager, who promptly stomped on it.

"Get them!" Natalie Buckmaster yelled. She led the other kids in flailing around at the imps who were dragging Michael.

"Ali! Use your magic," said Jennifer.

"You can help, too," Ali said.

"Come on!" Jennifer cried. "We all have magic." She grabbed hands with Molly and Tyler.

Ali looked around the whole room. There must have been fifteen "adults" and at least as many kids packed into the tiny room, all involved in the highly ineffective brawl. She focused on the overgrown imps. "WIGS OFF!" she yelled.

Fifteen wigs shot off of fifteen heads and stuck to the ceiling, joining Pilose's wig.

"My hair!" wailed the man who'd had the pink bows.

At the same time, something pulled on Ali's back. She had forgotten all about Hannah's arm around her. Now she grabbed it and pushed it off. With a loud sucking sound, the fake, rubbery Hannah whooshed up to the ceiling and stuck there with a splat. A second later, the fake Deacon hit the ceiling, making a whoopee-cushion fart sound.

"You stinky little pig!" he whined.

"WHAT is going on here?" a voice cried.

The mayor pushed her way between two imps who were un-acrobatically jumping to retrieve their wigs. The mayor's husband hurried in behind her. All the imps stopped jumping or crying or giving children noogies and looked down at the ground.

"The children came for the In-betweens, just as you thought," said Pilose, crawling out from under the table, dragging Natalie Buckmaster by her shorts.

"Well, well," said Bunny. "These children will come in quite handy for my new spell."

"We're not going to let you do any spell," said Ali.

"Yeah!" said Michael from the ground, where four bald adult-size imps were sitting on him.

"You'll change your tune when you hear what the spell is," said Bunny. She adjusted her Raggedy Ann wig. "I may have overestimated the joy of being a parent. I've created an un-parent spell that will duplicate the bodies we inhabit. That way, you children will get your parents back, and we will finally be rid of all ties to you. I suppose you like that idea as much as we do."

Ali did like the sound of that, but she didn't trust Bunny. "We don't trust you," she said. "And what about Hannah and Deacon? Where are they really?"

Bunny waved Pilose over, and the two imps had a whispered conversation.

"If the spell works," said Bunny, "and you don't interfere, we'll give you back the In-betweens. You can test them out to make sure they don't stick to the ceiling."

"Let us down, you little gremlin!" said the fake Hannah, kicking her rubber legs.

"How do we know your spell will work?" asked Ali.

Lockner grimaced and wrung his hands.

"I was chosen by the great Impoliptus himself to lead the Divvy-imps out of enslavement and into enlightenment," said Bunny, puffing her chest up.

Ali wasn't so sure she bought that. But it didn't matter, because all she had to do was get to the real Hannah and Deacon. Pretending to go along with Bunny was their best hope. "You're saying our parents would get their bodies back?"

"Absolutely," said Bunny. But it didn't escape Ali's notice that Lockner's face was frozen in an expression of despair. She bet that Bunny's new spell was as poorly thought out as the others.

"First, tell your imps to stop fighting with the kids," Ali said.

Bunny sighed. "Fine. Everyone let the kids go."

The imps who were sitting on Michael got up, and the rest let go of him.

"You'd better tell me what goes into this spell," Ali said.

"Well," said Bunny. "First we need some children. You all will do nicely."

"Children?" said Jonathan Yeager. "I don't think so." He pushed his way between Bunny and Lockner and left the party room.

"Fairies go home! Fairies go home!" the kids chanted, following Jonathan. One kid still had part of a posterboard sign—which now just read OME—and he waved it energetically.

"Seize them!" cried Bunny.

The "adults" raced out of the party room after the kids.

"Come on," Ali cried, waving at Michael. They followed Bunny and Lockner, who followed the imps.

"This isn't helping!" she called. The brawl was starting up again. Kids were grabbing wigs off the heads of the imps who were still trying to eat. Other wigs whooshed up to the ceiling.

The front door burst open. Mrs. Hopper walked through it. A wig hit her smack in the chest. She caught it and held it up, looking for the culprit.

"Oops, sorry," said Natalie Buckmaster.

"Don't be sorry. She's a fairy named Follica!" said Michael.

"My name is not Follica," said Mrs. Hopper, dropping the wig onto the ground. "I am the *real* Emily Hopper."

THIRTY-TWO

A boy Ali had never seen before came in the door. "That's her," said the new boy. "I want revenge on her!" He looked around the room. "And him!" He pointed at Jonathan Yeager.

Ali suddenly realized who he was. "Jared?" He had dirty-blond hair that hung over his forehead just so, and deep blue eyes, and pale, acne-free skin. Jared was now *really good-looking*.

"That's right," said Jared. "This fairy lifted my hex, and now she has to get revenge for me because I rescued her from the barber pole."

"What barber pole?" said Ali. "Wait a minute. Fairy?"

Bunny's eyes opened wide. She turned around and tried to get back into the party room, but Michael grabbed her by the collar and pulled her back. Bunny kicked, but Michael pulled her around to face Mrs. Hopper, who was slowly advancing, a wicked gleam in her pale old-lady eyes.

Lockner began to tiptoe toward a hallway at the side of the dining area.

"Not so fast, Lockner!" said Mrs. Hopper, pointing a bony finger at him.

Lockner dejectedly plodded back to stand next to Bunny.

"Who exactly are you?" asked Michael.

The kids and the overgrown imps shifted into separate groups again. Mrs. Hopper's authoritative-grandmotherness had taken the wind out of the fight.

Mrs. Hopper surveyed the room and reached a hand up to brush back her unruly, wiry mess of gray hair. "I *am* Emily Hopper," she said. "And yes, dearie"—she nodded at Ali—"I am a fairy. I suppose you children were foolish enough to believe these imps when they styled themselves fairies, as you humans do get your stories quite mixed up. Nevertheless, I can assure you that I am the real thing."

"Wait a minute," said Ali. "Are you really the real Mrs. Hopper, or did you take over her body?"

"This is my own body," said Mrs. Hopper. "I've been watching over this town for some time now. All was well until I was ambushed by these uppity Divvy-imps who don't know their place."

"Watching over us how?" asked Jonathan Yeager,

glaring at his now-very-attractive cousin, who tapped his foot impatiently, eyes shooting lasers back.

"When you come for your haircuts, I sprinkle you with a touch of health," said Mrs. Hopper. "I also ward off pesky sprites who might cause mischief, which I suppose is another reason these imps came for me. Aside from my delicious stash of hair clippings, of course."

At the mention of hair clippings, Ali's mouth watered. Was she ever going to stop craving hair?

"Who cares?" said Jared. "I want my revenge."

"Yes, yes," said Mrs. Hopper. She stood on one foot and pointed a long finger at Jonathan Yeager. "Make him as ugly as he made his unpleasant cousin."

In the next five seconds, a look of horror overcame Jonathan's face. Soon the same look was etched onto an acne-filled, grotesque-featured face being clasped in ungainly, pock-marked, fungus-fingered bony hands. "My face!" Jonathan howled. "Oh, it's not just my face!"

"Now her," said Jonathan, pointing at Ali.

"What? I didn't do anything to you!"

"You said you'd give me your fairies and you didn't. I was supposed to get my wish, but you lied to me."

"You've got your looks back," said Ali. "And I would have given you the fairies if I had them. I didn't know they were going to do the parents-replacement spell. I didn't get my wish either!"

"She makes a good point, dearie," said Mrs. Hopper.

"I don't care what she says," said Jared. "You promised me revenge."

"Hmm, I did promise," said Mrs. Hopper. "But I think I've paid you back enough. You did deserve that hex, you know. No, I'm not going to hex the girl. I'm going to set things right."

"How exactly are you going to do that?" Ali asked.

"Easy enough, dearie," said Mrs. Hopper. "I'll cast the Divvy-imps out of your parents' bodies. Then I'll return all the children to their natural states—except that boy, of course." She pointed to the sobbing Jonathan Yeager. "He's rightfully hexed. I'll return the rest of you to your natural states—as if the imps never were un-enslaved—and then—"

"Hey!" said Jennifer, jumping up onto Ali's shoulder. "I got my wish fair and square. You can't take my good looks away from me!"

"And look how it turned out for you," said Mrs. Hopper.

"It turned out fine," said Jennifer. "It'd be nice of you to make us big again, but you have no right to take away our wishes."

"Yeah," said Natalie Buckmaster, pushing in front of Jonathan. "We earned them."

"That's right," said Michael. "I grew my fairies—I mean imps."

"They earned their wishes," said Ali, thinking that she'd earned hers too and then some. She'd definitely never trust a magical creature ever again. She'd learned that the hard way. *Maybe I did get a little smarter,* she thought.

"The imps should never have offered wishes," said Mrs. Hopper. "Bargaining with children is unnatural—it upsets the balance of just deserts. No, I'll return the children to their natural states and erase their memories of the whole sequence of events. Everything will go back to normal."

The kids burst into protest. "Erase our memories? She can't do that!"

Ali agreed. She wanted her parents back, but there had to be some other way. No one was going to take away their hard-earned wishes or erase their memories if *she* had anything to do with it.

"Erase our memories!" said Jared. "I never agreed to that!"

"Shut up, dearie," said Mrs. Hopper.

"No, I will *not* shut up!" Jared yelled. "Listen up,

everyone. We've got magic ourselves. She called it child magic, and all I had to do was rub my head with my writing hand and hold my foot with the other hand." He demonstrated, hopping and nearly falling.

Child magic, thought Ali. Of course the imps had failed to tell the kids *that.* She had lots of reasons not to trust Jared, but the angry look on Mrs. Hopper's face confirmed that he was telling the truth.

"Quick, do it!" Ali shouted. "Everyone!" She whipped off her own shoe and sock.

Michael pushed Bunny away and did the same.

Ali, who was left-handed, rubbed her tuft of hair with her left hand and grabbed her left foot with her right hand. She had to think of some words to say, fast. "Repeat after me . . . um . . ." *Hair. Hair. No,* not *hair.*

"Run away fast!" Michael shouted.

That was it! "Run away fast!" Ali repeated.

The other kids joined in. Ali felt the power around them—a glowing aura. It was holding them up on their single legs, helping them balance, directing their energy against Mrs. Hopper.

"Children change back!" cried Mrs. Hopper, balancing effortlessly on one foot.

Jared ran to join the other kids. "Run away fast," he yelled.

"Children change back!"

"Run away fast!"

Ali was starting to sweat. Neither side seemed to be winning, and even with the "child magic" or whatever it was, balancing on one foot wasn't easy. She couldn't keep this up forever.

"Louder, everyone!" Michael boomed. "Run away fast! Run away fast!" All the kids shouted together at the top of their lungs. It was so loud that Ali wanted to cover her ears or run away herself, but she yelled along with the rest of them.

"Children—" Mrs. Hopper began. "Oh! Oh!" Her other foot dropped to the ground. She leaned forward and clenched her fists as if fighting against a giant wind.

"Run away fast!" the kids shouted.

She spun around and crouched down like an Olympic sprinter on the starting block.

"Run away fast!"

Bang! Mrs. Hopper bolted through the door and ran into the street. As she ran, her hair came off of her head and landed in a gray pile. Bald-headed, she ran straight through the parking lot of the auto shop across the street, and in only a few seconds, she was out of sight.

The kids stopped chanting, let their feet drop to the ground, and burst into cheers.

"And don't come back!" Ali yelled. She stared at Mrs. Hopper's lost wig. "Doesn't anyone around here have real hair?"

"I guess not," said Michael.

"La la laaaaa!" Natalie sang.

"And grow our luscious impy hair back!" a voice shouted.

"Who said that?" Ali asked, looking around.

"Oh no," said Michael. "Bunny must have done her spell while we were fighting Mrs. Hopper!"

There, over by the hallway that Ali supposed led to the kitchen, was Bunny in the bald, wigless body of the mayor. Next to her stood Lockner, holding the headless Happy Rat by his arms. Bunny pushed Hannah and Deacon in front of her. Both teenagers were wearing obvious wigs.

A series of popping sounds came from around the room. What had Bunny been trying to do? Duplicate all the parents so they could have bodies of their own.

Pop! A second mayor exploded out of the side of the first one. The second body didn't completely separate, though. Instead, it hung slack and unconscious from Bunny's side. The only apparent difference between the two bodies was that the copy had a thick head of red hair.

"Wake up, you idiot!" said Bunny, shaking the lifeless doppelgänger.

Pop! A second body sprang out of Lockner's back, toppling him with its weight. He flailed around like a tipped turtle.

"The wigs, Ali!" Michael cried. He raced toward his brother.

The wigs! Ali raced toward Hannah and collided with the speeding Michael. She fell backward onto her bottom. *Ouch! That really hurt.*

"Ali! Are you okay?" Hannah reached down to help her up.

Deacon reached down to help Michael. "Whoa, bad fall, bro."

Ali caught Michael's eye. As one, they grabbed for their siblings' heads. This time the wigs came off in their hands.

Hannah clasped her hands to her bare head.

Deacon's eyes opened wide.

"Noooooooo!" Bunny cried. She and the other "adults" vanished with a loud pop, lifeless duplicate bodies and all.

"What is going on?" the Happy Rat moaned.

"What have you done?" Bunny shrieked.

"We don't want to be small!" a voice cried from the floor.

Ali looked down. There were the imps, huddled together in a bunch, as tiny as they had ever been. Did that mean her parents were back in their bodies? She sure hoped so. And she hoped they had only *one* body each.

"Hair."

"Hair."

"Hair."

The tiny cries spread like a wave through the whole flock.

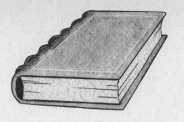

THIRTY-THREE

It WORKED!" Michael exclaimed.

"Where did everyone go?" asked the Happy Rat, rubbing his eyes.

"What happened to my hair?" Hannah asked, sounding more bemused than upset.

"I think your head looks beautiful," said Deacon, gazing down at her lovingly.

Ugh. Even under the influence of magic, those two had the power to make Ali sick. But she couldn't worry about that. Even though Bunny was small again, she could still be a lot of trouble. The imps could make all the kids small like Tyler and Molly and Jennifer. Tyler and Molly and Jennifer!

"Jennifer! Are you guys okay?"

"Not quite," came a squeak from behind Ali.

"Hold still," said Michael.

Ali did.

Michael plucked Jennifer from the back of Ali's shirt and set her back on Ali's shoulder.

"I could have been squashed!" she said.

"I think I was," said Tyler from the backpack.

"I'm sorry!" Ali cried. "Just hang on. We're still going to figure out a way to make you big again—with all your hair."

Just then, the front door burst open. Two tiny figures came into view. They marched into the middle of the room.

"Who are you?" Ali asked.

"I am Impoliptus," said one of the imps. His voice, though small, boomed through the room. "And this is my sister, Sky."

"See!" Sky cried, opening her tiny arms wide.

"The Great Imp!" a voice squeaked.

"The Great Imp!" other voices repeated.

"Where is Bunniumpton?" Impoliptus loudly demanded. "I surmise it was she who just attempted and botched an Un-Parent-Parent-Duplication-Un-Imptimization-Final-Freedom spell?"

No one answered.

"Why are there a bunch of wigs stuck to the ceiling?" asked Hannah.

"That spell is absolutely forbidden."

"Says who?" a tiny voice shouted.

"Says I, Impoliptus, as you well know, Bunniumpton. I made it perfectly clear to you what consequences you would face should you break the rules. There is a very clear warning in the front cover of the *Great Book of the Imps*, which Sky lovingly penned herself: 'No imps must attempt to grow big or interfere with the human world in any way excepting in their traditional role as divvy-outers of punishments and rewards.'"

"See!" said Sky, producing a tiny quill pen out of thin air.

"It's written right in the book?" Lockner's voice said.

"I'm not sure," said Bunny's voice. "Her handwriting is hard to read."

"Bunniumpton!" Impoliptus shouted.

No response.

"Down from the rafters, up from the floor, out of the closets into this jar!" Impoliptus declaimed. A glass jar with a lid appeared before Impoliptus and Sky. A faded and torn label on one side read FARM FRESH PICKLES.

Whap! Whump! Two imps clunked against the inside of the glass.

Bunny commenced jumping up and down and waving her arms about, but Ali couldn't hear a sound. The other imp, presumably Lockner, slumped against the side of the jar and covered his tiny ears with his hands.

"Looks like you're in a pickle now, huh, Bunny?"

Ali said. She stared down at Impoliptus. "Not that I care, but what exactly are you going to do with them?" She hoped he would take Bunny and go away, but she doubted it would be that simple. Getting rid of all the imps was going to be a lot harder than chasing off one real fairy.

Impoliptus raised his arms and jumped effortlessly up onto the back of a nearby chair. "Fellow imps, children," he said. He paused to point a thin finger at the jar, where Bunny was not losing any steam. "Holes," he said. At once, several holes appeared in the top of the pickle jar, and Bunny's screams came through loud and clear.

"Let me out!" she shouted, pounding on the side of the jar. "You're going to pay for this!"

"See!" cried Sky.

"See what your greed has done," said Impoliptus, glaring at the group of kids.

"Our greed?" said Natalie Buckmaster. "All we did was help *them*."

"Who would have grown a flock if not for the incentive of a granted wish?" asked Impoliptus.

The children grumbled.

"Imps and children," Impoliptus continued, "are bound together for their own protection. Imps must be bound to children because left unchecked, their evil natures will cause chaos. Children must be bound to imps because without some check on their greedy natures, they will grow up to be awful people."

"Not Virginia," Bunny squealed. "That child wouldn't harm a blade of grass!"

"Yeah, if you're evil, don't you want people to be awful?" asked Michael.

"When evil is truly in your heart, you do not need to feel it from others," said Impoliptus. "True evil is more precious when not shared."

"What a load of crap!" said Bunny.

Impoliptus ignored her. "The rules that govern me require that I test my charges once every five generations, if they ask. The legends that precede even us"—he opened his hand to indicate his sister—"declare that one day, the imps will be ready for un-enslavement, that they might perpetrate their evil without bestowing it on the undeserving. When the imps are ready, the legends say that a new sprite will take care of children. So when Bunniumpton came to us, I had no choice but to give her the secrets of un-enslavement, so that you imps could be tested. You have failed miserably and, I fear, are no nearer to being ready for the freedom to work your own evil than you were all those many generations ago when you spent your days tormenting sea creatures and humans alike."

"Pilose, where are you?" Ali called. "You never told me you tormented sea creatures!"

"You never asked," Pilose said. She was standing at the

back of the pack of imps, not far from Ali. "Besides, that was before my time."

"You would have done it if you could, you—"

"Having failed the test," Impoliptus continued loudly, "you will be re-enslaved for another five generations."

Bunny slammed herself against the side of the jar. The jar toppled over. "I'm not going back to that child!" she shouted. "I'd rather be bald and eat hair for the rest of my life!"

"I just want to go home," said one of the imps.

"My Peter was very naughty," said another. "I miss him."

"But children are so big!" squealed a baby.

"It will be all right," said Pilose. "When we're Divvy-imps again, they won't be able to hurt us. They won't be able to see us or know we're there."

"Wait a minute," said Ali. "We want the imps to go away. We don't want them to go back to being our Divvy-imps. Nobody gets to decide whether we deserve rewards and punishments except for us. And maybe our parents, but you can always get out of things your parents say."

"Rewards and punishments? What are you talking about?" asked Natalie.

Ali turned to the kids. "These imps used to go around hurting us if we supposedly did something wrong and helping us if we were 'good' — before Bunny did her spell and made it so we could see them and they had to eat hair. Now they want to go back to being invisible and knocking us down stairs and things."

"Let's stomp all over them," said Jonathan Yeager, wrinkling his pustule-covered nose.

"Yeah," said Natalie Buckmaster.

Michael looked uncomfortable. "I can't squash them after they gave me a wish."

"Then don't," said Jonathan. "There are plenty of us who can."

"We can't kill them," said Ali. "It's them who're evil, not us."

"Does anyone care that we're still small?" cried Molly from the top of Ali's backpack. "There are three of us down here. We've been slaves and had to cover seashells with mousse all day and night. We've had to eat hair, and no one's fed us any all day!"

"You did break the rules," said Impoliptus, "but your punishment has been just. Very well."

"Alison, you might want to put them down on the ground," said Pilose.

Ali held out her hand for Jennifer, Tyler, and Molly to climb on and gently set them down in front of her.

"See!" cried Sky. Then she and Impoliptus chanted:

"From children once, they became small. They children were and still they are. Justly punishment now done, it's only fair they not crave hair. HAIR!"

All of a sudden, there were three full-size kids standing in front of Ali.

"I'm me!" Molly exclaimed. She patted her hair, which was back in the imp-protective bun.

"And I'm me!" said Tyler. The two of them hugged each other with joy.

Jennifer stood regally, radiating beauty. She reached up to her head and began taking pins out of her luxurious blond hair. "I don't care whether it makes you crazy or not," she said, dropping the pins on the ground. As they clattered to the floor, the imps crowded around her feet.

"Hair!"

"Hair!"

"Hair!"

"Yes, it is," said Jennifer, shaking out her hair so that a few strands fell to the ground.

The imps pounced on them. More and more piled on, desperate for a taste.

Ali saw her opportunity. All the kids were back to normal or better now, except Jonathan Yeager, who deserved the hex-back anyway. She still had only the tuft of hair, not a whole imp's worth of magic. But they had just gotten rid of Mrs. Hopper using "child magic"—something they were supposed to have had all along.

"Come on, Michael," said Ali. "We're not going to stomp on them, we're just going to send them away too." She took his hand and looked up at him (way up).

Michael's face turned beet red. "O . . . okay," he stammered. "What are we supposed to do?"

The imps jumped around Jennifer's feet. She leaned over and shook her hair vigorously. The imps jumped for the strands, but being unable to grab on to any, they kept falling back on top of one another.

"Everybody grab hands," said Ali. "Let's concentrate our magic."

"We should do the thing we did before," said Jared. "Rubbing our heads and hopping on one foot."

"That's what Mrs. Hopper told you to do," said Ali. "I bet she didn't want you to use all of your power. I think there's a better way." She knew she had to get it right the first time, or the evil imps could be around forever. This was the real test—Mrs. Hopper had just been practice.

"We have more magic than you," said Impoliptus. "It will be better if you let Sky and me perform our ritual and accept things the way they were."

Ali suddenly realized where she could find the answer. With the hand not holding Michael's, she pulled the directions out of her back pocket.

THIRTY-FOUR

Give me that paper," said Impoliptus.

Now Ali was *sure* the directions could help her. "This paper has to tell me the truth, doesn't it?" she said. "It's linked to these rules you all keep talking about."

"That's my handwriting you see," said Sky. "And my exquisite illustrations. You are only seeing what I write."

"Then you have to write the truth, and all I have to do is ask," said Ali. "Kids got tricked into breaking the rules because they never thought there might be more directions, or they didn't ask the right questions. If I ask the right questions, then I win. All I have to do is be smart." *And I* am *smart,* Ali thought. *I've gotten us this far.*

"You will be in grave danger if you do not give me that paper," said Impoliptus.

"I don't think so," said Ali.

"We still have the power to grant your wish," said Impoliptus. "You have grown your flock, and it was not fair for Bunniumpton to deny you your reward."

"I don't need you to grant me a wish," said Ali. "I'm already smarter than Hannah and smarter than you." *Now prove it, Ali,* she told herself. She looked down at the paper and thought carefully. What exactly did she need to know? "What are *all* the rules for using child magic?"

Impoliptus pointed both hands at Ali and began whispering. At the same time, Sky pulled a tiny quill out of her pocket and began writing on air. The paper fluttered in Ali's hand.

Child Magic may only be used to affect sprites, plants, and inanimate objects. (Sprites = all magical creatures human-sized or smaller, including imps, fairies, djinns, pygmy unicorns, and some trolls.)

You must never attempt to use Child Magic to affect humans, other animals, or non-sprite magical creatures.

The power of a child's magic increases exponentially when combined.

To combine with greatest efficiency, link together like this:

* Areas of greatest magic

Children ↑

TO CAST A SPELL

1. Touch fingernails and toenails together (touching the toenails of one child to another's creates more power. Each child should touch his or her own fingernails together).
2. Concentrate mental energy on the hair follicles.
3. Speak words describing the desired outcome. Rhyming is always helpful.

"Confound it, Impoliptus!" Bunny cried, now pounding on the upturned side of the pickle jar. "Can't you get those directions away from her?"

"It's your fault she has imp-powered hair on top of her child magic, Bunniumpton," Impoliptus snapped. "I suggest you help me stop her." The jar lid popped off, and Bunny and Lockner scrambled out.

Swoosh, swoosh. Four of the girls from the group of kids followed Jennifer's lead and let their hair down. They swung it back and forth over the leaping, fighting pile of imps.

"Hair," said Lockner.

"Focus, Lockner," said Bunny. She jumped up to the back of the chair where Impoliptus stood.

"See!" cried Sky, jumping up to join them.

"Shut up with that already," said Bunny.

"I just want to be a Divvy-imp again," said Lockner. "I'm sick of this." He leaned toward the girls, who were still energetically swooshing their hair.

"All right, everybody look at this," said Ali. She held the directions up. "We're supposed to link arms . . . and take your shoes and socks off first so we can press our toenails together."

"Let's make them small," said Bunny.

"Four imps can't make a child small," said Impoliptus, "and the rest of your Kingdome is overcome by the filamentous biomaterial."

"What?" asked Bunny.

"Hair!" Lockner squeaked, leaping off the chair. He landed on the floor with a little bounce and raced into the pack.

"Well, we have to do *something!*" Bunny cried.

Impoliptus shook his luscious black imp hair. "We can undo the un-enslavement spell. That will return you to your bonded homes and make all Impdom right again."

"No." Bunny folded her arms.

"The children are about to attempt a total displacement," said Impoliptus. "There's no telling where you'll end up. And no doubt your craving for hair will be unabated. Do you want to find hair to feed two thousand imps every day for the rest of your lives?"

"We'll find another salon," said Bunny.

"And were the imps happy there, in your Kingdome?" asked Impoliptus. "Without homes of their own? Without roast beef and mashed potatoes?"

"No," said Bunny. "But they'd be happy living on the beach like the ancient imps. Undo my mistake with overdoing the hair. Let them be un-enslaved."

"They have failed the test," said Impoliptus.

"No they haven't," said Bunny. "I have. Let them go free."

"They are not ready, Bunniumpton. They must wait five generations."

"I won't help unless complete freedom is our goal," said Bunny. She turned away from Impoliptus and folded her arms.

"Fine," said Impoliptus. He winked at Sky behind Bunny's back. "Let's plan our spell."

"Okay," said Ali. She had linked one arm with Michael and the other with Natalie Buckmaster. The other kids had attached themselves to the chain, which snaked around behind Ali, except for the five girls who were distracting the imps by shaking their delicious hair.

"We'll have to help you from here," said Jennifer, dropping a single hair onto the flock, grinning as the imps jumped for it.

"Do you think you can fix me?" asked Jonathan, whose back was pressing into Ali's.

"I don't know, but I'll try," she said.

"Thank you," said Jonathan.

"Will you kids please leave?" asked the Happy Rat, who was dejectedly holding his ruined head.

"I think we'd like a hamburger," said Hannah, sidling up next to him. "We've just eaten at Mom's Crab Shack, but for some reason I'm hungry again."

"Mushroom burger with extra fries," said Deacon.

"Please, just leave," said the Happy Rat, on the

verge of tears. "First a whole bunch of crazy people eat everything in my kitchen and take over my party room. Then a bunch of kids come in, start a brawl, and destroy my dining room. Then, poof, all the adults disappear and the kids start talking nonsense about growing vegetables. Why didn't I just go to college?" At that, the Rat broke down and began to sob.

"Quick," said Michael. "Those imps are about to do something."

Impoliptus, Sky, and Bunny were huddled together on the chair back, whispering.

"Focus on your hair follicles," Ali called out. "And repeat after me." She didn't know what she was going to say, but she had to trust that her imp magic and her child magic would tell her. The words were there in her brain, waiting to pop out. She just had to let them flow. She pulled Michael's and Natalie's arms in tighter, and suddenly there was a connection. It was as if they were all thinking as one. And the words appeared in Ali's mind.

The children chanted:

> "We are children.
> We are strong.
> We won't be punished.

Right or wrong.
Imps have no right to choose our fate,
To give us things or take away.
We make our choices for ourselves, and
We will make our own rewards.
We have magic
More than yours, so
With this rhyme we cut the cords!"

The three imps (Bunny, Sky, and Impoliptus) pointed at the children and chanted:

"Some are naughty

Some are nice

Some are almost six feet high

Children bound us

Good and bad

But good outweighed and

Made us sad

Rewards weighed on us

Harms were few

We'd rather torment crabs

We rue

The day we bound ourselves to YOU!"

The children chanted:

> "Leave this town
> And don't come back.
> Don't touch us,
> Write,
> E-mail,
> Text.
> We never want to hear from you
> In any way ever again
> Don't call until
> The world ends!"

And the imps chanted:

> "Send us home to sandy shores.
> We'll never cross a child's door.
> We only want to frolic free
> Back near where
> Our Sky shouts, 'See!'"

"See!" shouted Sky.

Ali blinked to clear her vision. While they'd been chanting, the room had become a pale haze. Now it was clearing, and all the imps in the room began to glow. Suddenly, she was filled with dread. How could she have forgotten? "Crista!" She grabbed Jennifer by the arm and pulled her aside.

"Hey!"

"Crista!" Ali shouted. "Crista's still down there. We're sending her away with the rest of them." She fell to her knees and scanned the pack of imps for Crista, but all the imps looked the same. Why didn't she come out?

"Crista!" Michael got down next to Ali, and so did Jennifer.

"Crista, come out!" Ali cried. "Please! You aren't really an imp. Please answer me!"

The glowing from the imps got brighter and brighter and became a shining red. *Poof!* It flashed so bright that Ali had to cover her eyes. When she removed her arm, every single imp was gone.

THIRTY-FIVE

"CRISTA!" Ali shouted to the empty space. "She can't be gone. She's not supposed to be an imp. She's supposed to be with us." If she'd had her hair back, she would have torn it out. Instead, she leaned over her knees and grasped onto the bald edges of her head.

"Woo-hoo! We did it!" someone cried.

"Great job, Ali!" Natalie Buckmaster slapped Ali on the back. "La-LA-LAAAA!" she sang out, proving her diva singing voice was still there. "You've gotten rid of them *and* we kept our wishes!"

"A-li! A-li! A-li!" the kids chanted.

"Why don't you guys just go home?" said Michael, resting one giant hand on Ali's back.

"Let's go back to school and make sure our real teachers are there," said Molly.

"Good idea," said Tyler. "Since my parents apparently forgot about me, I guess they can wait."

"Thank you, Ali," said Molly. "We owe you."

"A-li! A-li!" the kids kept chanting as they walked out of the restaurant.

"You're gonna pay for this, Jared," said Jonathan.

"Serves you right," said Jared.

"Oh yeah?" The cousins pushed through the door and took their argument out into the street. Michael and Jennifer stayed with Ali, while Hannah and Deacon held hands and gazed into each other's eyes.

"Please!" cried the Happy Rat, twisting his ruined head. "Please just leave. I have to get this cleaned up before my boss comes in."

"We're sorry," said Michael. "Come on, Ali, let's go back to your house. Maybe we can figure it out from there."

Ali let him help her up.

Jennifer gracefully picked up a table and set it upright.

"It's all right," said the Happy Rat. "I'll do it. Please just go."

"Come on, Hannah," said Ali. "Let's go home."

"Okay," said Hannah. She picked Deacon's wig up off the floor and set it back on his head.

He picked hers up and set it on her head. "Beautiful."

Leaning on Michael, Ali headed for the door.

"Ali, wait!" said Hannah, running around in front of her. She held up a wig with thick, straight brown hair. "This one would look wonderful on you. You can't go around almost bald." Her superior tone sounded like the old Hannah, before she was addled by a combination of magic and love. Ali almost smiled as Hannah set the wig on her head and adjusted it. "There!"

Hannah took Deacon's hand and led the way out of the restaurant.

It was a long walk home, and nobody said much. Hannah and Deacon went off on their own, and Ali led Michael and Jennifer up to her room.

"I'm sure there's a way to find Crista," said Jennifer. "We'll do another spell. One that locates imps or something."

"I guess," Ali said. "But why didn't she answer me? Why didn't she jump out of the pack? She doesn't even want to come back, and it's my fault. *I* got her turned into an imp."

"I wonder if they'd trade my wish for her," said Michael. "I don't mind being my old self again."

"Unfortunately, that's not possible," said a voice.

Ali looked around for it. There on Ali's desk stood Pilose. She looked the way she had in Ali's vision back in the mound—complete with long, flowing imp locks.

"Pilose!" Ali cried, running over to her. "Tell me where Crista is!"

"Pilose?" said Michael. "Where is she?"

"Right here on the desk," said Ali, pointing right at Pilose's head. "And she's got her hair back."

"I don't see anything," said Michael.

"Me neither," said Jennifer.

"Well, she's right here," said Ali. "Didn't you hear her speak?"

Both of the others shook their heads.

"They won't be able to see or hear me," said Pilose. "You see, our spells didn't quite work out. Apparently you and Bunny wanted the same thing—to set us free from each other. But Impoliptus tricked Bunny, and it turns out we're Divvy-imps again. The other children can't see us because only you have a remnant of imp magic."

"Divvy-imps again!" Ali cried. "What about our child magic?"

"You tried valiantly," said Pilose, "and you helped re-enslave us. But it's difficult to get out of just deserts."

Ali rolled her eyes. The whole "just deserts" thing. "Are you my Divvy-imp, then?"

"No, Alison," said Pilose. "This imp is yours now." She waved a hand toward the back of the desk.

Another imp moved slowly out from behind the pencil case. There was no mistaking the pink T-shirt and the long brown hair. It was Crista.

"Crista! You're my Divvy-imp? No way."

"Crista is right here? And *she's* your Divvy-imp?" asked Michael, leaning over Ali in a fruitless attempt to see.

"It's all right," said Crista. "I am what I am now. And we have a whole 'nother year together before you get too old and I have to bind to another child."

"A year." Ali pushed a strand of wig hair out of her face. "We'll figure out a way to help you. I promise. Can you at least eat real food now?"

"Yes," said Pilose. "One good thing about this whole mess is that we're no worse off than when we started. Bunny is back with Virginia, and that child is punishment enough for an evil imp. Well, Ringlet and I have children of our own to deal with. I'm sure I'll see you again."

"Wait!" Ali cried. "You have to help Crista! And you have to turn me back to normal." She pulled off her wig, exposing her fairy hair tuft. "Plus Hannah's and Deacon's hair."

"Everyone's hair will grow back," Pilose said.

"Am I supposed to *wait* for it to grow back?" Ali asked. "You imps can make it grow back right now."

"Sorry," said Pilose. "By myself, I don't have that kind of power." *Pop.* Pilose disappeared into thin air.

"Wait!" Ali cried, but it was no use.

"It'll be okay," said Michael. "It won't take that long."

"It's not just my hair," Ali said. "She must know how to help Crista. I don't believe for a minute that it can't be done." She picked up the directions, which she had dropped on the desk. "How can I turn Crista back into a person?" She waited. Nothing happened.

"I think it was tied to the un-enslavement spell," said Crista. "And that's undone now."

Ali let the paper fall to the desk. "I just wish I had my wish," she said. "Then I'd be able to figure this out, no problem." She sat down in her desk chair and dropped her head onto her hand.

"You don't need a wish to be smart, Ali," said Crista. "That's what I was trying to tell you at the beginning. Look at what you did. Yeah, some stuff went wrong, but you figured it out. You got everyone's parents back, and the kids got to keep their wishes and their memories, and there won't be any more hexes, and now we don't have to eat hair. Even the imps are better off because of you."

"You're already a rock star," said Michael. "Remember how all the kids chanted your name?"

"I guess," said Ali. She *had* done a lot. She'd saved Hannah too. "But if you have to stay that way, it's not enough."

"I have faith in you," Crista said. "You'll figure out how to change me back eventually. But I'm fine for now. There are some good things about it." She grinned and waved a hand.

Ali's chair flew out from under her and she landed on her bottom.

Michael, Jennifer, and Crista all burst out laughing.

"Hey!" Ali cried, staring up at Crista. "Did you do that?"

"That's for getting your best friend turned into an imp," Crista said, winking. "And you'd better be a good girl this year, because that was only a stage-one punishment."

Ali scrambled to her feet. "Now I'm *really* getting you turned back," she said.

"Ali!" her mother called from downstairs. "Help me bring these groceries in!"

"Just a minute!" Ali called.

"Maybe your parents will remember something,"

said Jennifer. "Like, maybe they'll have some *sense* of how you saved them even if they don't *know*."

"Alison Elizabeth Brown Butler!" her mom called.

Ali rolled her eyes. "Yeah, maybe."

All four of them—three kids and an imp—laughed.